MURDER IN THE MISTLETOE SHOPPE

THE KITTY WORTHINGTON MYSTERIES, BOOK 11

MAGDA ALEXANDER

CHAPTER 1

LONDON, 1924

AN EARLY DECEMBER MORNING

"*Y*ou'll need to bundle up, darling," Robert Crawford Sinclair, my newly minted husband, exclaimed as we made ready to leave our cozy townhome on Eaton Square. "It's a bit nippy out there."

"A bit nippy!" I said. "It's freezing."

"Thus, the need to bundle up," he said with a crooked smile.

Mister Black, our ever so efficient butler, and Grace, my lady's maid, stood in the foyer with our winter garments. Once we'd donned our coats, hats, gloves, and scarves we stepped out the door and headed toward Robert's Rolls Royce.

Thankfully, his manservant, Hudson, had already done the work of bringing it around to the front of the house, so all we had to do was make our way to it. But even in that short distance the morning air, crisp and sharp as it was, stole my breath away.

"Ready?" Robert said as I sunk into the passenger seat.

Trying hard to keep my teeth from chattering, I replied, "As I'll ever be."

He grinned. "Your nose is red."

"I don't know why they can't put heat into automobiles."

"One day they will, but for now, you'll have to make do with me."

Taking him up on his invitation, I snuggled as close as I could to him. It warmed my right side but did nothing for my left.

"Comfy?" he asked.

"Yes." I was extremely grateful for his body heat and luscious scent.

He now drove me every morning to the Ladies of Distinction Detective Agency claiming it was the least a loving spouse could do. While I thought it very sweet, it was rather impractical as I needed my roadster to tool about town. But since it was winter and the temperatures were beyond frigid, I was not about to complain. If I needed to do a spot of investigation or meet with a client, I could always hail a taxicab.

Traffic was light that morning. So in no time at all, we pulled up to the agency. Anticipating the warmth that awaited me inside, I quickly kissed him goodbye and stepped out of the automobile. As I rushed toward the agency's entrance, I inhaled the scent of roasting chestnuts in the air. The aroma added a festive touch to the streets. Undoubtedly, December had arrived, and with it, the promise of a holiday respite. All we needed to do was wrap up our current investigations.

The agency's brass plaque gleamed in the wintry morning sunlight, a beacon of professionalism in the bustling city. Filled with energy for work and eager to dive into the day's cases, I pushed open the door, setting the small bell above it jangling. I was greeted by Betsy, our ever-efficient receptionist and part-time bookkeeper, who was already perched behind her desk diligently reviewing the morning correspondence. Smiling warmly, I said, "Good morning, Betsy."

"Good morning, Lady Robert," Betsy replied, her voice as bright as her expression.

The honorific sounded harsh to my ears. But because I was now Robert's wife, and he was the heir to a marquessate, etiquette demanded I be addressed in such a manner. But in my heart of hearts, I was still Kitty Worthington.

After tucking my kid leather gloves into my satchel, I removed my coat and hat and hung them neatly on the stand by the door. The agency's offices, situated in an elegant Georgian townhouse on Hanover Square, exuded the warmth of polished wood and tasteful decor. Mother, who loved to redecorate, had donated several pieces and my brother-in-law, Sebastian, a noted botanist, had gifted us several plants. Our reception area was not only elegant but comfortable, attributes which our clients truly appreciated. I took a moment to savor the ambiance before heading into the office of my partner, Lady Emma Carlyle, where she was waiting to conduct our scheduled meeting. Our weekly discussions were a vital ritual for the agency, a time to review our cases and strategize for the days ahead. It was also an opportunity to reflect on our successes and plan for the agency's growth.

It didn't surprise me to find her seated at her desk, a stack of case files neatly arranged before her. She was never less than efficient. As I entered, she glanced up with a welcoming smile. "Good morning, Kitty." She knew how I felt about 'Lady Robert,' so she always made a point of referring to me by the name I preferred. In return, she'd requested I call her by her given name, Emma, and drop the lady. Of course, I'd agreed.

"I trust you had a pleasant drive?" she asked.

"Quite pleasant, thank you. The streets are beginning to feel festive, though the chill is unmistakable," I replied, taking my seat across from her.

Emma's demeanor turned brisk as she handed me a steaming cup of tea. "Perfect weather to keep us indoors and focused on our work then. Although we've made significant progress on our caseload, there's much to discuss."

I nodded, as I retrieved a notebook from my satchel. As usual, Emma began by outlining our current caseload: a mix of delicate society matters, business disputes, and a few lingering assignments for prominent solicitors.

"The good news," she announced, "is that we're on track to wrap up all our cases before the Christmas holiday. A few require follow-up interviews and paperwork, but nothing too demanding. It's remarkable, really, considering the volume of work we've had this year."

"That *is* wonderful news," I agreed. "It will give us all a chance to enjoy the holiday season without the weight of unresolved cases."

"Indeed." Emma hesitated, her expression thoughtful. "The agency's success has presented a new challenge, though. We've grown so popular that we can no longer keep up with the demand. As we discussed, we'll need to hire additional help at the start of the new year."

After I returned from my honeymoon, Emma had made that point blatantly clear, so it was not unexpected. But we hadn't had an in-depth discussion about it until now. "What sort of help are you considering?"

"Two positions," Emma replied. "First, Betsy has been doing an admirable job managing both the reception desk and some of my bookkeeping duties. But it's more than one person should handle. I'd like to promote her to full-time bookkeeper, which will free me to focus solely on investigative work. That means we'll need to hire a dedicated receptionist."

"An excellent idea," I agreed. "Betsy is meticulous with the accounts. She's taken to it like a duck to water. Not only that, but her evenings are spent studying accounting instruction manuals."

"During her luncheons as well," Emma pointed out with a smile. "Just the other day I caught her in our library boning up on Elementary Accounting Principles."

I grinned. "Better her than me. I've never had a head for figures."

"Your talents lie in other areas, Kitty."

"I do like to snoop." We both broke into laughter. "But I agree about Betsy. We'd benefit greatly from her full attention in that area. We should give her a raise as well." Betsy was engaged to Neville, the Worthington family's chauffeur. His ambition was to open a motorcar repair business. Father was floating him a loan so he could establish his shop in the spring. With Betsy's increased salary, they could move into their own cozy home. But only if they so wished. Right now, they both resided at Worthington House. In separate rooms, of course. Heaven forbid they should engage in any hanky-panky at Worthington House.

"Precisely," Emma said, her tone approving. "Now, the second position would be for another lady detective. Even with the addition of Lady Aurelia, as wonderful as she has been, we can't keep up. The sheer volume of cases has been overwhelming at times. Another associate would considerably lighten the load. I'd like someone experienced, if possible, but we will need to train them in our methods."

One possibility immediately jumped to mind, but first I needed to clarify one thing. "You don't think we need to consider a man for the detective position?" Although we'd never discussed it, I feared that might be a deficiency in our staffing. Not that I believed gentlemen were superior. As far as I was concerned, ladies could do as good a job, or better, than a man in our profession. Still, I felt I should mention it.

Emma's lips quirked in an amused smile. "While I see the logic, our agency's name *is* the Ladies of Distinction Detective Agency. Our clients come to us specifically because they trust us to handle their matters with discretion and understanding. Adding a male detective might disrupt that dynamic. If a gentleman is truly needed to perform a particular matter, we do have Mister Clapham."

A former detective inspector at Scotland Yard, Mister Clapham brought a unique set of skills. I'd first hired him to teach me investigative techniques. When Emma and I opened the agency, he was our first hire. We'd never once regretted that decision.

"I wholeheartedly agree we should only consider ladies." After pausing for a moment, I said, "I do have someone in mind for the new lady detective position."

"You do?" Going by her wide-eyed expression, Emma's curiosity was piqued. "Who might that be?"

"Ummm, I'm going to keep that under my hat for the moment, if you don't mind. I believe she will be perfect, and this is something she wishes to do. We'll have to train her, though, as she has little experience in the field."

"That's no impediment, Kitty. After all, we had to train ourselves."

"I'm glad you agree with me," I said. "She's very bright and, as I said, eager to perform detective work. Between the two of us and Mister Clapham, she'll learn in no time."

"Whatever would we do without him?"

"We certainly would not have achieved the level of success we have. We owe a lot to him."

Emma took a sip of her tea. "As far as the new recruit, you're confident she'd be a good fit?"

"Absolutely," I said with conviction. "She's not only clever but also eager to learn. And an excellent listener, which is invaluable in our line of work."

"Very well," Emma said with a nod. "I trust you. Could we arrange an interview for the first of the year then? I'd like to talk to her before we reach our final decision."

"That should prove no problem," I promised, already envisioning how our new hire could contribute to the agency.

The discussion turned to the practicalities of hiring, including advertising for the receptionist position and arranging interviews. Lady Emma emphasized the importance of finding an individual who not only possessed the necessary skills and temperament but also shared the agency's values of discretion and professionalism.

As our meeting concluded, I felt a renewed sense of purpose. The Ladies of Distinction Detective Agency was thriving, and the coming year promised even greater challenges and opportunities. With the right additions to our team, we would be well-equipped to handle whatever cases came our way. I couldn't wait to see what the future held for our growing enterprise.

Even as I gathered my things to head to my office, the agency telephone rang. Another client, I thought, as I wondered whether we could take on another enquiry. But happily, it was Mother eager to discuss our holiday plans.

CHAPTER 2

SUNDAY SUPPER AT WORTHINGTON HOUSE

*E*ven though the cold December winds rattled the windows of Worthington House, warmth reigned in the drawing room. The Worthington family and friends—including Robert and me, of course—had once again gathered for Sunday supper. A crackling fire in the hearth lent its welcomed heat to the space as we conducted a spirited discussion about our holiday plans. Everyone, especially Mother, was excited the entire family would spend Christmas together. We hadn't done so in such a long time with Richard having been away in Egypt.

The only person missing was Robert's brother, Lord Rutledge. His heart condition had flared in recent months, causing frequent spells of breathlessness. Though Robert tried not to show it, he was deeply worried about him. During supper, he'd reached for my hand under the table when his brother's name had been mentioned. I'd squeezed it back, silently communicating I was there for him and that everything would be all right.

Our holiday plan was to travel in a week's time by railway to Winchester where motorcars would whisk us to Wynchcombe Castle, my brother-in-law, the Duke of Wynchcombe's, family seat. Last year all of us, sans Richard, had enjoyed the wonderful Christmas festivities, as well as celebrated Sebastian and Margaret's wedding day. There had been a minor hiccup in the way of a body we'd discovered. But we'd managed to solve that murder in time for the nuptials. So, in the end, all had been well. This year, we did not anticipate anything getting in the way of our holiday celebration. Or at least, I prayed there wouldn't be. We all deserved a vacation from the many murder investigations.

"You'll enjoy your time at Wynchcombe Castle, Richard," I said, trying to jolly him out of his foul mood. Two months before, my brother had arrived home deathly ill with malaria. He'd recuperated nicely, as far as his physical being was concerned. The same could not be said for his mental state, however.

"Will it be warm there?" After spending several years in Egypt's hot climate, he'd found it difficult to reacclimate himself to the cold English weather.

"Inside, of course," Sebastian said. "I installed central heating in all the bedchambers."

"You have to make an effort, dear," Mother said, sitting beside Richard. As always, she exuded a gracious composure. She was the peacemaker of our family, the one who quietly ensured everyone felt cared for.

Richard came to his feet. "I've done nothing but, Mother. I miss . . . the sun." Richard had worked several years as an archeologist, something he adored. But his physician, an expert in malaria, had pretty much put the kibosh on him returning to Egypt. If he did, Richard was bound to suffer another relapse which might very well kill him. The forced stop to his career weighed heavily on him.

"The sun will return in the spring," my sister Margaret said, no doubt in an attempt to improve his mood. "And it will be glorious."

"If you say so," Richard said as he moved closer to the blaze in the hearth.

"How are the preparations going?" I asked Sebastian, eager to shift the limelight away from Richard. "We'll be quite a large retinue."

Sebastian inclined his head. "Indeed. The staff at Wynchcombe Castle has been hard at work preparing the rooms. The courtyard and Great Hall will be decorated with festive greenery, wreaths, and other adornments. Megs and I have also planned a sleigh ride, a dance, a visit to the church to listen to the children's choir, and, of course, the Christmas feast."

My heart gave a little leap at the thought of the bustling castle at Christmas. The scent of pine, the crisp winter air, and the echo of holiday merriment reverberating through ancient stone walls—there was a special magic to Wynchcombe Castle during the holidays. I glanced toward Margaret, sitting quietly gently caressing her belly. Sebastian, protective as ever, slipped his hand over hers.

"Last but not least, the trimming of the Christmas tree," he said.

As we'd discovered last year, part of that activity included a drinking game which made the hanging of ornaments via a very tall ladder a rather perilous affair.

"I'm looking forward to that bit of merriment," Margaret exclaimed.

Sebastian's head swiveled toward her. "Your feet will not be leaving the ground, Megs."

Margaret pouted. "Why not?"

"Because you're seven months along, that's why. I'm not about to put your life and that of our unborn child in danger by letting you climb a ladder."

"Even if I'm on the first rung?"

"Even so."

"Spoilsport," she said with a grin. Margaret recognized that Sebastian was being overprotective which made sense given it was their first child. She neither resented it nor denied him. She believed everything would turn out fine in the end.

While they continued their back and forth, I approached the trio of Father, Ned, and Robert who were deep in conversation at the other end of the room. As soon as I joined them, Robert welcomed me by curling an arm around my shoulders.

"He needs an occupation," Ned said in a conspiratorial whisper.

No guessing who 'he' was.

"With his expertise, he would be a great asset to the British Museum," Father said, "but he refuses to talk to anyone there. I arranged for an interview with the curator of Egyptian antiquities, and he failed to show up. All he wants to do is sit home and sulk."

"He can't go on like this," Ned said in a slightly louder voice.

"May I say something?" Robert asked.

"Of course," Father said.

"I was in a similar situation after I recuperated from my injuries from the Great War. Lord Rutledge—"

"Your brother," Father said.

"Yes. I only thought of him as a friend as I had no knowledge of our familial connection at that time. Well, he arranged for me to interview at Scotland Yard for a detective position. I turned it down. What would be the good of such a thing, I thought, since I was returning to the front?"

"Whyever did you wish to return, Robert?" I asked. "You'd already paid a horrible price." His injuries had been so extensive, it had taken him months to recuperate.

"I believed that was where my duty lay, Catherine. I couldn't very well remain in the safety of home while others were suffering through that horrible war."

"So, what changed your mind?" Father asked.

"Lord Rutledge made me see there was a great need at Scotland Yard. So many men had joined the army, that it had decimated its ranks. They were in desperate need of able-bodied men with police experience."

"And because you'd been a police officer for a number of years, you were a great asset," I said.

"Yes. He convinced me I could provide a much-needed service here in London."

I squeezed his arm. "And you did."

"Yes. I believe so." He lovingly gazed at me before glancing back at Father. "The point I want to make as far as Richard is concerned is that you could appeal to that side of him. Anything Egyptian is currently all the rage. With his expertise and practical knowledge, he could give talks not only at the British Museum but also at the Royal Geographical Society. He would be quite the draw."

"My ears are burning. Are you perhaps discussing me?" A peeved male voice asked. Unnoticed by us, Richard had made his way across the room.

"We were," Father said, owning up to it. He'd never been one to lie.

"Maybe I should join the conversation then," Richard said, not angry exactly, but definitely perturbed.

"By all means," Robert said in a calming tone. Leave it to him to become the peacemaker.

"I'll leave you to it, gentlemen," I said. This discussion was best held between the four men. Richard would not appreciate his younger sister telling him he was acting like an idiot.

Noticing Hollingsworth was seated by himself on one of the settees in the room, I headed in his direction. I hadn't seen him since Paris when he'd helped us solve a murder. After Robert and I returned from the City of Light, we'd been so busy doing, well, what newlyweds usually do that we hadn't invited anyone to our home. Hollingsworth had also been missing from Mother's suppers as well. So, this was a wonderful opportunity to catch up. "Mind if I join you?" I asked.

"Of course not." I expected a quip along with that dazzling smile of his. But oddly enough, he appeared quite morose. How very odd.

Taking the space next to him, I asked, "How are the plans for your next expedition coming along?"

He took a long sip from his whiskey glass before he answered, "They're not."

Well, that was alarming. For the last year, he'd been fitting his ship for his next seafaring adventure. Whatever could have happened? "What do you mean?"

"I've stopped the improvements to the sailing vessel."

"Why?"

"I won't be sailing anywhere in the near future."

"Why not?"

"Reasons."

Good heavens! He was being very obtuse. "What reasons?"

"None that I can share or that you need to know." He abruptly came to his feet. "Excuse me. I believe I'll make my goodnights." Putting action to words he approached Mother. After a quick conversation, he did the same with his sister, Mellie, and then he was gone.

What on earth was going on with him? Robert didn't know. *If he did, he would have told me. Or would he?*

But I had no more time to ponder about Hollingsworth's odd behavior when Margaret sat next to me. "A penny for your thoughts."

When I explained about Hollingsworth, she said she'd noticed his state of mind as well. But she had no clue any more than I did as to the reason for it. I would mention it to Robert. They'd been friends since their Oxford days, and Hollingsworth had been the best man of our wedding. If anyone knew what the matter with him was, it would be Robert.

A smiling Lady Lily soon joined us. Margaret's sister-in-law, affianced to my brother Ned, was smiling from ear to ear. Not a surprise. Since her engagement to Ned, she'd been incandescent with joy. She was not only gaining a husband she adored and in turn adored her, but she was gaining a family, something she'd sadly lacked while growing up.

"How are the wedding plans coming along?" I asked. The wedding day was set for June.

"Everything's right on schedule."

"Has Mother introduced you to the joy of the wedding planning album?" I asked.

Lady Lily grinned. "And several folders. I keep up with it daily. The church—St George's at Hanover Square; the flowers; the wedding gown, the trousseau. Oh, and the invitations. I just received them this morning. Can you believe we're inviting over 600 guests?"

"Well, you are the sister of a duke and marrying the junior partner at Worthington and Son, the best investment firm in the City of London."

Lady Lily trilled with laughter. "I would marry Ned in sackcloth and ashes in the smallest church in the city. All I want is to be his wife."

I pressed her hand. "We can't have that. Not as beautiful as you are."

Lily blushed. "I don't hold a candle to you or Margaret."

"Me?" Margaret said patting her stomach. "I'm as big as a house at the moment. And getting bigger by the hour."

"Pshaw," I said. "Impending motherhood suits you." She radiated the healthy glow of an expectant mother seven months along.

"Oh!" Margaret put a hand to her burgeoning stomach and shifted in her seat.

Sebastian who'd been watching her closely quickly approached. "Anything amiss, dear?"

Margaret shook her head. "It's just your son trying to make room." She turned to me. "The midwife thinks it will be a large baby which makes sense given Sebastian's height."

Sebastian's brow furrowed. "Are you certain you're really up for the trip to Wynchcombe, my dear?" Some found him imposing by virtue of his title and stature, but he had a gentle heart—especially when it came to Margaret. Clearly, he was worried about Margaret's well-being as our planned journey grew near. "Dr. Jameson advised caution in these final months."

Margaret looked at him with soft defiance. "I'm fine, Sebastian. Truly. I couldn't imagine missing Christmas at Wynchcombe—especially not when our child is already such a part of our family tradition."

Though Sebastian nodded, I could practically see his unresolved worry. "If you're sure," he conceded, "then we'll go. But if you feel the slightest hint of discomfort, you must tell me. Train travel can be rough this time of year, and the cold air is bitter."

Mother, who'd overheard the conversation, set out to reassure Sebastian. "We'll make sure the train compartment is well heated. And we'll have blankets, plenty of them. Margaret will be properly looked after."

The conversation between the men seemed to have ended. A happy conclusion had not been reached if the expression on their faces was anything to go by. Curious as to what had been determined, I excused myself and approached Robert. He greeted me by resting his hand reassuringly at the small of my back. Grateful for it, I leaned into his warmth. But before I had a chance to ask anything, a footman appeared in the doorway.

After a quick glance around the room, he approached Robert. "Lord Robert, there's a telephone call for you. It's Lord Rutledge's physician."

Robert's shoulders tensed. "Excuse me." Wasting no time, he followed the footman into the corridor. The chatter in the drawing room stilled, as we all held a collective breath. My hands twisted. I knew how precarious Rutledge's condition was. Any 'turn,' as they called it, could prove disastrous.

The moments crawled. I heard the faint murmur of Robert's voice in the hall where the telephone was located but couldn't discern the words. I glanced from one anxious face to another—Mother, breathless with worry; Father, lips pressed together; Margaret and Sebastian, holding hands. The hush was stifling.

Robert came back, pale as the moon. He strode to my side and spoke in urgent, clipped tones. "Rutledge's physician says he's had a serious turn. I must go to him immediately."

My heart clenched. "I'll come with you."

"No, my darling," he said, a firm kindness in his eyes. "It may be a long night, and who knows what I'll find once I get there. Let me go. If I need you, I promise I'll send word."

I wanted to argue—my instincts were to be by his side. But the look he gave me held both love and a protective resolve. Feeling my pulse hammering, I managed a nod, though my heart twisted painfully.

My family surrounded Robert then, each offering encouragement or quick embraces. "Please let us know anything as soon as you can," Mother whispered, resting a hand on his shoulder.

He gave a solemn nod. "I will." And with that, he hurried out, calling for his coat and hat. A moment later, the front door closed behind him, and the night swallowed him up.

CHAPTER 3

A WEEK LATER

A CHANGE OF HOLIDAY PLANS

As I approached the townhome Robert and I shared, snow swirled through the brisk December air, settling in soft drifts along the street and frosting the iron railings. Normally, the sight of such a winter wonderland would have filled my heart with anticipation for the days to come. But today, I felt the ache of disappointment.

The door to our townhome suddenly opened. Not a surprise. I was expected after all.

"Good evening, milady." Our butler, dressed in traditional livery, held himself with dignified grace and impeccable posture just inside the threshold. While his neatly combed silver hair thinned slightly at the crown, his face was lined with the marks of a lifetime of quiet service.

"Good evening, Mister Black," I said, handing him my hat, coat, scarf, and gloves.

Robert joined me at the door, his tall frame silhouetted against the soft glow of the interior. "Good evening, my dear.

I'm glad you are home," he said, kissing my cheek. "Have you wrapped up your last enquiry?"

"Yes. Finally." The agency had taken on a last-minute matter which had seemed simple at first but turned out to be a bit more complicated. Emma had offered to handle it, but I'd volunteered for the task. I was staying in town after all. No sense in her missing the holiday celebration at Wynchcombe Castle. She'd been looking forward to it as much as I had. Not eager to return tomorrow to write the report, I'd remained late to finish it. I'd left a note on Betsy's desk to mail it to our client in the morning, along with the invoice for the hefty fee he'd agreed to pay. That would be her last task before she and Neville made their way to Yorkshire to join his family for the holidays. The agency would be closed until January 3.

"I'd planned to be sipping mulled wine by now," I murmured. "In the warmth of Wynchcombe Castle, surrounded by family." It had been a week since we'd learned Robert's brother had taken a turn for the worst. It wasn't entirely unexpected. He suffered from a heart complaint. But the timing was perfectly awful. My entire family was celebrating the holiday at Wynchcombe Castle. But because of Lord Rutledge's illness, we had to remain in town.

Robert's expression was apologetic as we drifted toward our cozy library, but there was a firmness in his gaze that I recognized well—it was the look of a man shouldering a heavy burden.

"Catherine," he said gently, "I know this is far from what we'd hoped for, but my brother needs us here. With the doctors uncertain . . ." His voice trailed off as he shook his head. "Family must come first."

Ashamed of my outburst, I said, "Oh, Robert. I apologize. I'm being such a beast."

He captured my hand and drew it to his lips. "You could never be such a thing, darling. You're simply being human."

I rested my head against his chest. "I don't deserve you, Robert."

He kissed the top of my head. "I don't know what I'd do without you."

I glanced up at him. "Lead a calm and measured life, more than likely." Heaven knew I'd gotten into more than one scrape.

He fake shuddered. "Heaven forbid."

I squeezed his arm lightly as I regained my composure. "Not to worry. I've always loved London at Christmas. There's a certain magic in the air, don't you think?"

Robert's lips quirked into a smile, though it didn't quite reach his eyes. "You're remarkable, you know that?"

"I have been told once or twice," I replied, accompanying the teasing words with a smile.

We stepped into the warmth of the library, where the crackling fire in the hearth provided a cozy reprieve from the cold outside. It was lovely, of course, but it wasn't Wynchcombe Castle. There were no towering trees glittering with ornaments, no boisterous laughter echoing through grand halls, no Christmas carols being sung by a choir.

This Christmas would be different. But different, I decided, didn't have to mean disappointing.

I turned to Robert. "We'll just have to bring the magic here," I announced, my tone resolute.

Robert arched an eyebrow at me. "Here?"

"Yes," I said, already forming a plan in my mind. "If we can't go to Wynchcombe, we'll make our own little slice of it right here in London. A grand tree, festive decorations, carols—everything."

He studied me for a moment, his expression caught

between admiration and amusement. "You've made up your mind, haven't you?"

"Absolutely," I replied, slipping my arm through his. "Now, do try to keep up. We've much to do, and Christmas is but a few days away."

THE FOLLOWING MORNING BEING SATURDAY, I rose early, determined to set my plan in motion. While Robert attended to matters concerning his brother, I embarked on a mission to transform our London home into a haven of holiday cheer. I began with the kitchen, consulting with Cook to plan a menu worthy of a grand Christmas feast. Puddings, mince pies, roasted goose—each detail was meticulously considered.

Next came the decorations. I envisioned garlands of holly and ivy draped along the banisters, the warm glow of candles casting flickering shadows on the walls, and, of course, a magnificent tree to serve as the centerpiece of our celebrations.

For the tree, I ventured to Covent Garden, where the market buzzed with holiday activity. Stalls overflowed with wreaths, baubles, and trinkets, while the scent of pine and roasting chestnuts filled the air. I wandered among the vendors, selecting ornaments and ribbons with care, my spirits lifting as I imagined how beautiful it would all look.

"Kitty!" A cheerful voice called out, interrupting my reverie.

I turned to see Lady Delphine, an Oxford acquaintance, weaving through the crowd toward me. Her cheeks were rosy from the cold, and her smile was as splendid as ever. I'd first met her when Robert had been accused of murder. Her assistance had been invaluable in clearing his name. She'd had an ambition to open her own modiste shop. After that investigation concluded, she'd successfully convinced her father to foot the bill.

"Lady Delphine!" I exclaimed, delighted. "What brings you here?"

"I could ask the same of you," Lady Delphine replied, planting a kiss on my cheek. "I thought you and Robert were heading to Wynchcombe Castle."

My smile faltered slightly. "Plans have changed, I'm afraid. Robert's brother's health has taken a turn for the worse, so we'll be staying in London to be near him."

Lady Delphine's expression sobered. "I'm sorry to hear that. How is Robert holding up?"

"As well as can be expected," I said. "He's worried, of course, but he's doing his best to stay strong for his brother's sake."

"And you?" she asked, her tone gentle.

For a moment I hesitated before offering a small smile. "I'm determined to make the best of it. We'll have a wonderful Christmas here in London."

Lady Delphine nodded, her admiration evident. "If anyone can pull it off, it's you." Big Ben, which was nearby, suddenly chimed the hour. "I must run. I have a supper engagement."

"Who with?" I asked, curiosity getting the best of me.

"Oh, no one you know," she grinned. "So good to see you again, Kitty." After one more kiss on the cheek, she was gone.

BY THE TIME I returned home that afternoon, I had acquired not only the decorations I needed but also a renewed sense of purpose. After enlisting the help of the household staff, we transformed our home into a veritable winter wonderland.

Garlands adorned every available surface, candles flickered warmly in every room, and the centerpiece tree, resplendent with ornaments and ribbons, stood proudly in the drawing room.

When Robert returned that evening, he paused in the doorway, taking in the transformation. His eyes widened slightly, and for the first time in days, his smile was genuine.

"Catherine," he said, his voice filled with awe, "it's . . . perfect."

I crossed the room to him, a touch of playful pride in my step. "I told you, didn't I? We'll have a magical Christmas, no matter where we are."

He pulled me into a gentle embrace, pressing a kiss to my lips. "You're remarkable," he said again, his voice tinged with emotion.

"And don't you forget it," I replied, though my voice softened as I rested my head against his chest.

As THE DAYS TICKED BY, the warmth of the holiday season began to settle over our home. My efforts to create a festive atmosphere brought a sense of comfort and joy, not only to Robert but our staff. They seemed buoyed by the cheer, their laughter echoing through the halls as they prepared for the holiday.

But even amidst the joy, there was an undercurrent of tension. Robert's frequent visits to his brother's bedside left him weary, the strain of it visible in his eyes. I did my best to support him, offering quiet reassurances and moments of levity whenever I could.

One evening as snow continued to fall outside, we gathered in the drawing room. I had arranged for a small group of carolers to perform for not only us, but the entire staff.

Their voices filled the room with melodies that spoke of peace and goodwill. Robert sat beside me on the settee, his hand clasped in mine, and for a moment, the worries of the world seemed to melt away. Once they ended their concert, Robert and I withdrew to the library, our own cozy space.

"Thank you, Catherine," he said quietly, his voice filled with sincerity.

"For what?" I asked, turning to look at him.

"For everything you've done. For reminding me that even in the midst of uncertainty, there is still joy to be found."

My heart swelled at his words, and I leaned my head against his shoulder. "Always, my love."

I felt a deep sense of gratitude—not just for the warmth and beauty of the moment, but for the strength of the bond I shared with Robert. Together, we would face whatever challenges lay ahead, knowing that love and hope would always guide us home.

CHAPTER 4

A GRIM DISCOVERY

The soft glow of electric lamps illuminated the cobblestone streets of London, casting warm halos of light on the festive wreaths adorning shop windows. The Mistletoe Shoppe stood out among them all, its grand window displays a feast for the senses. Strings of fairy lights twinkled like stars amidst an array of handcrafted ornaments, miniature sleighs, and intricate snow globes. They not only sold holiday decorations but toys and games as well. Robert was a puzzle enthusiast, so I was here to see what I could find for him.

A subtle aroma of pine and a more exotic scent greeted me as I pushed open the door, the delicate chime of a bell announcing my arrival. Inside, the shop was a wonderland of holiday magic. The shelves overflowed with treasures: crystal icicles, velvet stockings, and wooden toys painted with precision. I let out a contented sigh. If ever there was a place to ignite the Christmas spirit, it was here.

"Good evening!" I called out, expecting to see either the jovial shopkeeper or his assistant bustling about. But strangely enough, only silence greeted me.

How very odd! It was unlike either of them to leave a customer unattended. They were well known for their effusive chatter and infectious holiday cheer. I stepped further inside, the soft rustle of my coat and the tap of my low-heeled boots the only sounds. I spotted a display of delicate marionettes hanging in a neat row and smiled. Mister Arkwright had a knack for selecting the most whimsical pieces. I reached out to inspect one when something caught my eye—an odd angle of shadow behind the counter.

"Mister Arkwright?" My voice wavered slightly as I leaned over to peer behind the counter.

My breath caught in my throat. There, sprawled on the floor, lay Arkwright, his ruddy complexion now pallid. His once lively eyes stared vacantly at the ceiling. A trickle of blood stained his skin from his lips to his chin. Unless I was very much mistaken, the shop owner was very much dead. Not only that but I strongly suspected he'd been murdered.

"Eloise," I cried out. Surely his shop assistant could not be far. When she didn't respond, I came to the realization I was quite alone. Surely, whoever had killed him would not have stuck around. Or so I told myself.

Careful not to disturb the scene, I scrutinized the body. I touched his hands which were clutching a small exquisitely carved, wooden marionette. A name quite familiar to me was etched into its base—*Hollingsworth*.

Oh, dear heaven! Could that name be referring to Robert's best friend? If so, how could he be tied to this grim scene?

I stepped back and scanned the shop. The front door had been shut when I entered, that much I knew. I distinctly remembered the sound of the latch as I walked into the store. There were no immediate signs of a struggle, but a faint metallic tang in the air suggested something more sinister than a natural death. Certainly, the trickle of blood hinted at murder.

My first thought was to telephone Robert. He was a Chief Detective Inspector at Scotland Yard, after all. But I knew time was of the essence. A local police officer needed to be alerted to the scene. As luck would have it, a constable appeared just at the street corner, more than likely on patrol. I hurried out the shop door toward the young man and explained what I'd seen. Moments later, he followed me back to the shop, his face blanching at the sight of Arkwright's lifeless form.

"Wait here, ma'am," the constable stammered, as he darted outside to summon additional help.

While he was gone, I used the brief respite to gather my thoughts. Why would Mister Arkwright be holding a marionette, and why would it bear Hollingsworth's name? I considered my friend's background. His explorations often unearthed rare artifacts, and his name was well-known in certain circles. Was it possible someone had sought to tarnish his reputation—or worse, implicate him in a crime?

Within minutes, the shop was abuzz with police activity. To my surprise, Robert arrived before too long. I hadn't called him. Had he been assigned to this investigation? His dark eyes narrowed in concern as soon as he spotted me standing near the counter.

"Catherine," he strode toward me, a look of worry on his face. "Are you all right?"

I nodded, though it was a lie. "I found him, Robert. He . . . he was already gone. And there's something you should see."

I pointed to the marionette, still clutched in the victim's hand. Robert knelt, his gaze sharpening as he read the name.

"Hollingsworth," he murmured. He straightened and fixed me with a probing look. "This could complicate things."

"I know," I said quietly. "But we both know Hollingsworth isn't capable of anything like this."

Robert's jaw tightened. "Even so, his name being here—on this—means we'll need to tread carefully. If there's a connection, Scotland Yard will find it."

I understood what he meant. "But not you."

"No. I cannot be assigned to this case, given his name is on that toy."

"Who then?"

"I don't know," Robert said. "It will be up to the superintendent to decide. But I can perform the initial investigation."

I prayed Inspector Bolton would not be assigned to this case. He'd arrested my future brother-in-law when his grandfather had been murdered. Not only had Bolton not looked beyond the initial facts, but he'd misconstrued a vital clue.

Soon, the shop was cordoned off, as Robert directed the team to begin a methodical search. I lingered, observing every detail. I noted the pristine condition of the shop—no overturned shelves, no broken glass. Whatever had happened, it hadn't been a robbery gone wrong.

An officer approached Robert with a preliminary report. "No signs of forced entry, sir. The shop's door readily opened."

"Have you examined the marionette?" Robert asked.

"Yes, sir. It's handmade. But no maker's mark exists, aside from the name carved upon it, that is. And that seems too crude. Someone who took such infinite care in creating the toy would have taken more care affixing his name to it."

But if Arkwright had done it while he was dying, he wouldn't have had the time.

Robert nodded, his expression grim. "Have the coroner

examine the body and the marionette. I want to know if there's anything unusual about either."

As the officers worked, my thoughts raced. If Hollingsworth wasn't involved, someone had gone to great lengths to implicate him. But why? Could it be tied to his last expedition? Or whatever was preventing him from going on the next one? He had encountered rival explorers—some of whom were less than scrupulous. Could one of them have done this? I needed more information, and there was one way to find out.

"Robert," I said, approaching him, "I think I should pay a visit to Hollingsworth."

He raised an eyebrow. "You're not thinking of conducting your own investigation, are you?"

"Of course not," I said innocently. "I merely want to check on him. If he's heard anything—or if someone's been asking about him—it could help. And he does need to be made aware of this." I pointed to the body that was growing colder by the second.

Robert sighed, well-acquainted with my tenacity. "Be careful, Catherine. And take Peters with you."

Peters, one of Robert's most trusted officers, appeared moments later, ready to accompany me. Together, we made our way to Hollingsworth's residence in a taxicab.

As I stepped out of the hired vehicle, I clutched the collar of my coat against the biting wind. Casting a quick glance up and down the street, I stepped up to the door. The polished brass knocker gleamed in the dim late afternoon light as I lifted it to make our presence known.

The butler answered promptly, his expression reserved. The moment he recognized me, his demeanor hardened like frost settling over glass. How very odd! He'd always offered me a warm welcome.

"Good afternoon, Lady Robert," he said stiffly.

"Good afternoon." I turned to my companion. "Officer Peters and I would like to talk to Lord Hollingsworth."

I could believe the butler could turn any stiffer, and yet he did. "I regret to inform you, Lady Robert, that Lord Hollingsworth is indisposed at the moment and unable to receive visitors."

I arched my brow, determined not to be deterred by the butler's frostiness. "I have no intention of taking up much of his time, but it is imperative that I speak with him. Might I inquire as to what ails him?"

The butler hesitated, his gaze shifting toward the hallway to his right. "I'm afraid I cannot say, milady. I must insist you leave—"

Before he could finish, a shadow wavered in the dimly lit foyer. Moments later, Hollingsworth himself appeared, swaying slightly and clutching the edge of the doorway for support. His normally impeccable attire was in disarray; his cravat hung loose, and his waistcoat bore the unmistakable stain of spilled liquid. His flushed face and bloodshot eyes told me all I needed to know. He was very much indisposed, just not in the manner the butler had implied.

"Why, it's Lady Robert in the flesh!" Hollingsworth's voice was a slurred echo of its usual sophisticated tone. Why had he called me by my formal name? He'd never once done that before.

He attempted a smile but failed miserably. "What brings you to my humble abode?"

With Peters close on my heels, I stepped past the butler, my sharp gaze taking in every detail of Hollingsworth's disheveled state. "What brings me here, Hollingsworth, is a matter of grave importance. May we speak privately?"

He waved a dismissive hand, nearly toppling over as he did. "Speak freely. What could be so urgent that it warrants a house call on such a dreary day?" His expression suddenly turned anxious. "Wait. Has something happened to Robert or Mellie?"

"No. They're both fine." Well, Robert was. I could only presume Mellie was as well. "It's Arkwright."

His gaze narrowed. "The Mistletoe Shoppe owner?"

"Yes. He's dead." I watched his face closely for any flicker of surprise, but Hollingsworth merely blinked, his sluggish mind seeming to struggle with the information.

"Arkwright . . ." he murmured, as though testing the name. "How terribly inconvenient for him," he said with an echo of his usual insouciance.

But this was no time to joke. "Hollingsworth," I pressed on. "When did you last see him? I know you've worked with him before, supplying artifacts to his shop. Did he contact you recently?"

He straightened, or attempted to, his bleary gaze sharpening for a fleeting moment. "Haven't seen him in weeks," he declared. "Months, perhaps. We aren't . . . bosom companions, you know."

I frowned. Something was deeply amiss, and it wasn't just Hollingsworth's state of intoxication. He was being evasive, far more so than usual, and there was a tremor in his voice that hinted at more than simple drunkenness. "Are you certain?" I asked softly. "Because if you're withholding anything—"

"Certain as the sun rising in the east," he interrupted, his voice defensive.

"There was something else. I found an object with your name on it in his possession."

Hollingsworth's expression darkened further. He leaned unsteadily against the doorframe, his brow furrowing as though trying to will clarity into his muddled thoughts. "My name? What sort of something?" he demanded, his tone veering between affront and curiosity.

"A marionette," I replied, my voice measured. "Hand-carved, with your name etched into it. Do you know anything about it?"

He stared at me, his bloodshot eyes blinking in slow succession as if the words needed time to settle in his mind. "A marionette?" he echoed, dragging out the word as if it were foreign. "No, never . . . never commissioned one of those. Why would I? I have no child." He swayed and made a vague gesture with his hand. "I've no connection to Arkwright beyond selling him a few artifacts from my travel and buying a few trinkets from his shop. Casual customer, that's all."

Peters, who had been quietly observing our back and forth, stepped forward. His voice was calm but firm, a stark contrast to Hollingsworth's erratic demeanor. "Have you noticed anyone acting suspiciously toward you, milord? Anyone who might bear a grudge or wish you harm?"

Hollingsworth tilted his head, squinting as if Peter's question required Herculean effort to comprehend. After a moment, he stroked his unkempt beard in what might have passed for a contemplative gesture if not for the drunken haze. "There was a fellow," he said slowly, "on my last expedition—a Frenchman named Dufresne. Haughty sort of chap, with a sharp tongue and an even sharper temper."

"What happened between the two of you?" I prompted, keen to draw more from him.

Hollingsworth let out a bitter chuckle. "We had a row over a rare artifact. A ceremonial mask, if I recall. He accused me of . . ." He hiccupped loudly and waved his hand as though swatting away an invisible fly. "What did he call it? 'Stealing the glory.' A load of rot, of course. Professional jealousy, nothing more. But surely, he wouldn't come all the way to England over a petty rivalry."

Peters glanced at me, then asked, "Where is this Dufresne now?"

Hollingsworth shrugged, nearly losing his balance in the process. "Haven't the foggiest. Last I heard, he was planning some grand expedition to South America. But that was months ago." He trailed off, his gaze drifting to the floor, where a decanter lay toppled on its side.

Peters made a quick note of the name in his pocketbook while my mind whirred with possibilities. Dufresne sounded like a plausible suspect—an aggrieved rival with potential motive and expertise in acquiring rare objects. If he were in England, he might well be connected to the marionette. But proving it was another matter entirely.

"Thank you, Hollingsworth," I said, though his contributions left more questions than answers. "Please do let me know if you recall anything else of significance."

"Will do." He hiccupped again. "Now, if you'll excuse me, I have . . . pressing matters to attend to."

Passing out came to mind.

As the butler stepped in, clearly intending to usher Peters and me out, I cast Hollingsworth one last scrutinizing glance.

Something gnawed at my instincts—a sense that his disarray was more than just personal indulgence. But for now, I had no choice but to leave. Outside, the cold wind bit at my cheeks, sharpening my resolve. The marionette was no mere curiosity; it was a clue, a breadcrumb leading toward the truth. Whatever shadowy path it marked, I would follow it to the end.

BACK HOME, I pored over my notes in my personal parlor, sketching a mental map of connections. The marionette,

Dufresne, and Hollingsworth. It all felt tangled, like a knot waiting to be unraveled.

Two hours later, Robert arrived, looking weary but determined. "The coroner suspects poison," he said. "Something slipped into Arkwright's tea, most likely."

I frowned. "Poison. Whoever did this must have planned it carefully and left the marionette as a message."

"Or a distraction," Robert said. "It's too early to tell." He brushed his knuckles across his brow. "Was Hollingsworth at home?"

"Yes. He was rather inebriated."

Robert's brow wrinkled. "That's not like him."

"That's what I thought. Shall I ring for something to eat? You missed supper."

"Yes, thank you. I was too busy to do so."

"I wouldn't want you to eat whatever can be found at Scotland Yard."

A sad sort of smile rolled over his lips. "It fills the belly whatever else it might be."

"Well, my darling," I said, curling my arms around his neck and kissing him, "we can do better than that." After I requested his meal be served in the library, we headed there where I shared what I'd learned from Hollingsworth. Robert planned to visit him in the morning. "Hopefully, he will be lucid by then."

"Has the superintendent assigned someone else to the case?"

"Not yet. He will do so as soon as someone becomes available. Many of the detectives are on holiday. In the meantime, I'm to keep meticulous records so that there will be no question of partiality."

"As if you would ever do anything else." I wrapped my arms around him. A murder investigation that clearly pointed to his best friend was the last thing he needed. "I'm sorry."

He hitched a finger below my chin and lifted it until I met his gaze. "For what?"

"For having to deal with this in addition to everything else."

He brushed a thumb across my cheek. "As long as you're by my side, I can handle anything that life throws my way."

I drew him down for a kiss. "Well, that's one thing you'll never have to worry about. I will always be there."

As he kissed me back, all the worry and sadness faded away. And after he ate his supper, we created our own little paradise.

CHAPTER 5

THE PRIME SUSPECT

The following morning, the chill of early December swept through London, carrying with it the sound of muffled conversations and the honking of horns. Inside our cozy townhouse, I paced up and down my personal parlor, flushed with indignation.

"Listen to this," I exclaimed, my voice rising as I read one of the morning papers.

Artifact Dealer Dead, Lord Hollingsworth Implicated in Mystery!

"They're making a terrible mistake!" Below the headline was an unflattering sketch of Hollingsworth, looking every bit the rogue the newspapers made him out to be.

"They're only reporting the truth, Catherine," Robert stated. He was sitting in an armchair, his brow furrowed as he reviewed the coroner's report that had been delivered this morning. Despite the warmth of the crackling fire, an unmistakable tension hung in the air.

"How did they even find out about Hollingsworth?"

"While we were examining the scene, a crowd gathered around the shop, including a few reporters. Someone may have accidentally revealed the carving on the marionette."

"Who?"

"I don't know. It could have been one of the coroner's men or a police officer. A press photographer was busy snapping photographs as well. These things have a way of leaking out."

I knew that as well as anyone. During many of the investigations I'd conducted, all manner of confidential information had made its way to the front pages of London newspapers. Still, I was right to be outraged. "Look at this one." My hands shook as I read from *The Tattler*, one of London's rags.

"Drunken Rage Murder?" A drunken quarrel between a certain peer and a holiday shop owner ends in tragedy when the shop owner is found dead—discovered, no less, by the wife of the peer's closest friend. Can justice prevail?'

I handed him the newspaper. "This one implicates you and me."

"That's rather unfortunate," he said, skimming the article.

"Unfortunate? It's disgraceful," I declared. "Not only have they turned him into a spectacle, but they've besmirched your reputation."

With a sigh, Robert folded the newspaper and set it aside. "This is what the press does best, I'm afraid. Scandal sells, and a titled suspect is precisely the sort of bait they dangle before their readers."

I stopped pacing and faced him. "They claimed he was three sheets to the wind. How did they even know he'd had too much to drink?"

"Someone must have walked into the shop and heard

Arkwright and Hollingsworth arguing. It's the only thing that makes any sense."

There really was no other explanation. "Hollingsworth wasn't in his right mind last night, Robert. You should have seen him—completely soused and barely coherent. He couldn't have orchestrated Arkwright's murder in that state."

"Perhaps not," Robert conceded. "But drunkenness doesn't absolve him of suspicion. You said it yourself—he was evasive. He told you he hadn't spoken to Arkwright for several weeks. The newspaper report seems to contradict that statement. There's more to his dealings with Arkwright than he's letting on."

I took a deep breath trying to calm the storm raging within me. Anger wouldn't get us anywhere. "That may be, but he's clearly troubled. There's a deeper story here, and we need to uncover it."

"I will. Peters should be here shortly," Robert said, glancing at the clock on the mantel. "We'll be paying Hollingsworth a visit this morning. Hopefully, he's sober by now. But drunk or not, he'll need to answer for what he knows. And," he added, his tone sharpening, "I need to find out why Arkwright's assistant was absent yesterday."

I nodded. "That was rather odd. All the times I've visited the shop she's always been there." An alarming thought suddenly occurred to me. "You don't think she's met with foul play?"

Robert shook his head. "She was seen leaving the store in the late afternoon on her own volition."

"Before I arrived then."

"Yes."

I perched on the arm of his chair. "Be careful with Hollingsworth. He may be acting out of character, but I suspect there's a reason for it. Probably one he doesn't care to reveal." Hollingsworth was often the life of the party, but he rarely shared anything personal. He was as deep as the sea he loved so much.

Robert placed a reassuring hand over mine. "I'll tread carefully. But this is a murder we're dealing with, and we can't afford to let sympathy cloud our judgment."

Before I could respond, the sound of the door knocker echoed through the house. Moments later, Mister Black's voice announced Peters' arrival. I stood, smoothing my skirt. "Good morning, Peters."

"Good morning, Lady Robert, Chief Inspector," Peters said with a slight incline of his head.

Robert had requested he be addressed in such a manner by Scotland Yard officers. I, however, could not avoid being called Lady Robert.

"Good luck, Robert," I said coming to my feet. "Give Hollingsworth my best."

He rose and kissed my cheek. "I will, my dear." Moments later, he and Peters were gone.

Today was Sunday, a day Robert and I usually spent with my family at Worthington House. But they'd already departed for Wynchcombe Castle, along with most of my close friends. The only one still left in town was Hollingsworth. Rather odd that. His sister, Mellie, had joined my parents in their travel. You'd think he'd joined them as well. Curious about his reasons for remaining in town, I yearned to question him. But I couldn't very well visit him again. Not today at least.

Nor could I visit Robert's brother, Lord Rutledge. He didn't wish me to see him as a frail, old man but remember him as the hale, hearty sort I'd known all my life. When Robert first told me, I'd resented it, but I had to respect his wishes. Not only for his own sake, but because he'd helped Robert in so many ways. My husband had achieved a great deal on his own merit. But without Lord Rutledge, he would have never attended Oxford nor joined Scotland Yard.

Lunch was a sad affair. Seeing as it was only me, I asked for the meal to be served in the library. Other than the bedroom Robert and I shared, it was the place I felt closest to him. I was just finishing my meal, when my bout of pity was interrupted by a knock at the front door, followed by the sound of Mister Black greeting the unexpected guest. Moments later, the butler stepped into the library and announced, "Lord Salverton, my lady."

Well, that was unexpected! I rose as the marquis stepped into the room. Tall and powerfully built, with blond hair and piercing blue eyes, Lord Salverton radiated an air of one in command. He was dressed impeccably, as always. But then he did have a role to play. I'd met him at Oxford during the murder investigation that implicated Robert. I'd suspected, and later confirmed, that he was a member of British intelligence. So, his visit begged the question—what was he doing here?

"Lady Robert," he greeted, inclining his head. "A pleasure to see you again."

After Mister Black cleared my luncheon dishes, I motioned for my newly arrived guest to take a seat. "Lord Salverton, what a pleasant surprise. Unfortunately, you've missed Robert. He's involved in an investigation." I didn't have to explain more than that. Salverton knew full well Robert was a Chief Detective Inspector at Scotland Yard.

"Yes, I know." Before I had a chance to ask him how he'd found out, he lowered himself into the chair opposite me. And then he glanced around the room as if assessing its suitability for their conversation. "It's not him I came to see, but you," he finally said, his voice measured.

"Me? Whatever for?"

"The unfortunate murder of Mr. Arkwright."

"Oh?" My curiosity piqued immediately. He not only knew about the toy shop owner's death, but that he'd been killed. But then he traded in information. "Did you know him?"

Salverton offered a faint smile. "Not personally, but professionally, yes. During the Great War, Arkwright served a vital role within the intelligence community. What I'm about to tell you is classified. You do remember signing the oath to the Official Secrets Act?"

"The one where I would be sentenced to life imprisonment if I disclosed any official state secrets? Yes, I remember."

"It's fourteen years, although life imprisonment can be imposed if the divulged information is serious enough. This matter meets that definition."

"Understood." Clasping my hands in my lap, I leaned forward. "I'm listening."

Salverton's gaze turned sharp. "Arkwright led a double life. While his shop served as a legitimate business dealing in holiday decor, toys, and curiosities, it was also a front for smuggling coded messages. He functioned as a courier for British intelligence, using the artifacts he sold as vessels for information. A seemingly innocuous trinket might have contained a cipher or a map, destined for allied agents in enemy territory."

I widened my eyes. "Fascinating. And dangerous, I imagine."

"Highly so," Salverton agreed. "Arkwright was skilled at navigating the shadowy world of espionage. To most, he appeared to be an eccentric shopkeeper with a penchant for rare items. But to those of us in the service, he was a critical asset, particularly in facilitating communications across enemy lines."

My mind raced. This revelation cast Arkwright in a

completely new light and deepened the mystery surrounding his death. "Do you believe his past work is connected to his murder?"

Salverton's expression darkened. "It's possible. While his involvement in intelligence work ended after the war, secrets from that era have a way of resurfacing. Old enemies, forgotten grudges—any number of factors could be at play. And then there's the matter of the marionette."

My pulse quickened. "I thought that was important."

Salverton nodded. "It is. I was briefed on the details this morning. The fact that it bears Hollingsworth's name is curious, but I suspect its significance goes deeper. Arkwright was meticulous in his work. If the marionette was left behind, it was likely deliberate. A breadcrumb, if you will."

My mind turned over the implications. "A breadcrumb left for whom, though. Hollingsworth? Or someone else entirely?"

"That," Salverton said, "is the question. Arkwright's network of contacts was extensive. During the war, he dealt with agents and informants. Any one of them could be involved. My presence here is not merely to share information, Lady Robert, but to request your assistance."

I blinked, surprised. "My assistance?"

Salverton leaned forward, his piercing gaze fixed on me. "You have a talent for unraveling mysteries and an ability to navigate social circles that are, frankly, beyond the reach of most of my agents. I believe you are uniquely positioned to investigate this matter discreetly."

I hesitated, my mind reeling from the unexpected turn of events. "I'm flattered by your confidence, but surely British intelligence has resources far superior to mine."

"Our resources are formidable, yes," he conceded. "But this is not a matter that can be approached with conventional methods. Arkwright's death is surrounded by secrecy, and any overt investigation risks exposing sensitive information. That's why I'm turning to you."

"Shouldn't you be turning to Robert?"

"Ah." He leaned back. "He will not oversee the investigation. In a few days, someone new will be assigned. More than likely someone who does not possess Robert's talents. The superintendent has asked Robert to keep meticulous records of the preliminary investigation, has he not?"

How on earth did he know that? "That's correct."

"If I sought his help, he would need to report it to the person who takes over the case. And that cannot happen. To put it mildly, Lady Robert, we don't know who we can trust at Scotland Yard."

"Do you mean to tell me there may be a foreign agent working there?"

"Maybe two. We suspect so, yes."

"How can that be?"

"During the Great War, so many men volunteered to join the army, the Yard was drained of capable individuals. Lacking sufficient manpower, they put out a call for new recruits. They didn't always apply the strictest standards to their new hires with the result some dubious characters slipped through. After the war ended and things returned to normal, the shadier ones were let go. But a few were too clever to get caught. We're hoping the investigation into Arkwright's murder will flush out the bad seeds." He paused for a moment as he fixed his gaze on me. "There is one more thing I must ask of you. I'm afraid you won't like it."

This would be even more daunting than what he'd already revealed. "What is it?"

"You can't tell Robert what I've asked of you, and you can't share your findings with him. You will only discuss what you discover with me."

After momentarily losing my breath, I asked, "I'm to keep my husband entirely in the dark?"

"Afraid so." Those two words turned my world upside down.

Coming to my feet, I paced the library trying to find the words to communicate how I felt. "Robert and I are husband and wife. We share everything, most especially our marital bed. Do you realize how difficult it would be to keep that information confidential? You are asking me to lie to him!"

"Not lie, simply not tell him."

I tossed my arms in the air. "There speaks the confirmed bachelor." Salverton had never married, nor did he intend to do so. He'd said as much.

"If you don't think you are up to it, you can refuse my request." A smile and a raised brow revealed his intent. He was daring me to turn him down.

I blew out a breath and took the conversation in another direction. "Robert will find out about your visit. How shall I explain it to him?"

"Tell him I came to inquire about the health of his brother. You offered me something to drink. Not tea. He'd never believe it."

"Whiskey, then." Putting action to the word, I poured a healthy measure into a glass and handed it to him.

He drank it down in one gulp. "Thank you."

I glanced at the clock on the mantel, my thoughts returning to Robert's interrogation of Hollingsworth. He would be returning soon. The time to accept or refuse Salverton's request was here and now. But I had little choice. This case had national implications. I couldn't turn it down. "Very well," I said at last. "I'll do what I can."

Salverton rose from his chair. "I expected no less, Lady Robert. I'll ensure you have access to whatever information you require. All you must do is ask." He retrieved a card from inside his coat. "This is my private number. If you have need of me, call it. An operator will answer. Tell him Lady Marigold wishes to speak with Bunny. Within an hour, I will return your call with a time and place for us to meet. Make sure you are alone at that time. Do you understand?"

"Yes."

"Repeat it please."

I did.

"Perfect. One more thing—trust no one. The world of espionage is fraught with deceit, and allies can become enemies in the blink of an eye."

"Understood."

Salverton inclined his head and took his leave, leaving me alone in the library once more. The weight of his words settled over me like a heavy cloak. Arkwright's death was no longer just a murder to be solved; it was a thread in a much larger tapestry of secrets and lies. And somewhere in that tangled web lay the truth about the marionette. I would not be able to share what Salverton was asking of me with Robert. But I intended to do everything possible to prove Hollingsworth's innocence.

CHAPTER 6

A HISTORY OF SECRETS

*A*n hour later, Robert returned, his expression grim as he entered my personal parlor. I'd been sitting at my writing desk, jotting down my thoughts in a new journal. As in previous cases, it would serve to keep track of evidence, clues, deductions, and conclusions. In other words, everything that had anything to do with the investigation. There was one major difference, however. I would need to keep it locked in my desk. Robert could never know what I wrote in it.

"How did it go with Hollingsworth?" I asked, glancing up at him.

Robert removed his gloves and tossed them onto a side table. "About as well as could be expected. He'd sobered up but unfortunately was quite belligerent at first. After much prompting, Peters and I managed to get a clearer picture of his relationship with Arkwright. It seems he's both purchased and sold several items from the shop over the years. But he insists he hasn't been there in weeks."

"Did you tell him somebody overheard his quarrel with Arkwright?"

"He swears it wasn't him."

"Do you believe him?" I asked.

Robert frowned. "He's hiding something, that much is clear. But whether it's connected to the murder is another matter." He ran a hand through his dark hair. "I hear Salverton was here."

"Yes. He came to inquire about your brother. I told him he was doing as well as could be expected. He said if you need anything, all you need to do is ask."

A frown wrinkled his brow. "What help could he possibly provide?"

I had to tread carefully. The last thing I wanted was to inflict more pain on Robert. "I imagine there will be steps involved in the transfer of the Rutledge title and the estate after—"

He cut me off. "I don't want to discuss that."

"No, of course not. My apologies." Better shift the subject to something mundane. "Have you eaten?"

"No."

"I'll ring for your lunch then. Do you want to eat here?"

"I prefer the library."

"Yes, of course. Why don't you head down there while I make the arrangements with Cook? There's a nice cozy fire burning in the hearth."

"I'll welcome that. It's beyond freezing outside."

I smiled at him. "I'll join you in a few minutes."

He nodded absentmindedly as he walked out the door.

A pang of guilt struck me as I locked the journal in my desk. I had never kept anything from Robert—at least, not since we'd been married. If he ever found out—no, better not think about that. I would make sure he never did.

Once I arranged for his meal, I rushed down to the library where Robert greeted me with an embrace and a kiss.

"Have I told you how beautiful you are?"

Wanting to change his somber mood to lighthearted, I teased. "Not lately, no. In Paris, it was a constant stream of I love you, *mon amour, ma belle* Catherine. But since we got back to London, not one word. Frankly, I'm beginning to feel neglected." I pouted even as I voiced that monstrous lie.

He captured my face in his wonderful hands. "*Mon cherie*, shall I demonstrate exactly how much I adore you?" He glanced side-eyed at the brown leather sofa that presided over the library, his meaning quite evident.

"Here? In the library?" I faked shock. "Mister Black will never recover!" More than likely our butler wouldn't turn a hair.

"Bother Mister Black." Even as Robert said that, our butler himself knocked on the library door which was wide open.

"Begging your pardon, Lord Robert, your luncheon has arrived."

Biting my lip to keep from laughing, I turned away while Robert directed the footman to lay the luncheon on a library table—beef stew accompanied by fragrant bread rolls, a bottle of burgundy, and a banana sticky toffee pudding for dessert.

"Thank you, Mister Black," Robert said once the deed had been carried out.

"My pleasure. Shall I close the door, milord?"

"Please."

It was only after the door was shut that I burst into laughter. "Oh, my," I said. "Do you think we'll live that down?"

"We weren't doing anything."

"But he must have heard us!"

"If the lord and lady of the house decide to cavort in the library, he's trained to see nothing, hear nothing." When I started to protest, he placed a finger on my lips. "Or even mention it."

"Yes, you're right. He is a treasure."

"That he is."

While Robert ate, I kept the conversation light and away from anything that would trouble him.

But when he was done, I deemed it time to return to the investigation. "Did you get a chance to talk to Eloise, the shop assistant?" It had been rather odd she'd been absent at the time Arkwright was murdered. But then maybe it wasn't. She could have witnessed the whole thing.

"Peters and I stopped at her address, a flat in Lambeth. We knocked, but she didn't answer."

"Could she have gone to the Mistletoe Shoppe? Maybe she was not aware of Arkwright's murder."

"If she had, she would not have been able to enter the store. It's closed for further investigation. We have a police officer guarding the premises. He would have notified me if she'd made an appearance."

"Where on earth could she be? We need to talk to her."

A crooked smile rolled across his lips. "We?"

"Well, you, of course."

"Of course," he said taking a sip of the burgundy. But the smile still lingered.

"So, what's next?"

"Two actuary officers are going through Arkwright's bank and shop accounts. If there's something there, they'll find it. I asked them to report their findings back to me by this evening. Tomorrow, Peters and I will be talking to the other shopkeepers in the area. Given the shop's prominence in the marketplace, somebody is bound to have seen or heard something."

"Hopefully."

"In the meantime, I'm going to visit my brother."

"I'd like to come with you, Robert."

He brushed a thumb across my cheek. "That's not what he desires, my dear. I'm sorry."

I swallowed back my disappointment. "Yes, of course. Give him my best."

"I will."

After he left, I returned to my parlor and wrote down what Robert had shared about Hollingsworth. Once I'd done that, I started to write questions for Salverton. Mainly, I needed to know what Arkwright had been involved in and who had been his associates. Although the shop provided an easy way for many people to come and go, there had to be at least one he trusted to be the go-between. Or so I thought. What were the signals they used to communicate? What kind of information was passed back and forth? More than likely, he would not be able to share most of the information, but some he would. And that would help. I was so absorbed in my task, I did not hear Robert enter the room. I quickly closed the journal and slipped it into a desk drawer. I would lock it later. He was bound to notice if I did it right now.

"Darling," I said, "How is your brother?"

"No better, no worse."

"Well, that's good. The better part I mean," I rushed to say.

"I know what you meant." He captured my face in his hands and proceeded to show me how much he cared for me. As he ended the kiss, he said, "Let's just talk about us, not the case, not my brother. At least for tonight. We can do that, can't we?"

I covered his hand with mine. "Absolutely, darling. Shall we make plans for our New Year's Eve celebration?"

"Dinner and the theatre?" he asked.

I curled my arms around his neck. "You've read my mind."

We spent the next hour discussing the merits of different entertainment. Just as we'd settled on an operetta, a messenger arrived from Scotland Yard. Not with the actuary findings but with news. Robert was no longer in charge of the Arkwright murder investigation, Inspector Bolton was.

CHAPTER 7

THE LADY IN THE WHITE FUR COAT

*A*fter Robert's removal from the Arkwright investigation, he was assigned to another murder that had taken place in St. Giles, one of the worst neighborhoods in London. That enquiry not only helped him from worrying about his brother but kept him unaware of my shadow investigation into Arkwright's death.

The next day, as I had no time to waste, I set off to find Eloise, the Mistletoe Shoppe's elusive assistant. She, more than anyone else, was likely to have vital information.

Robert had already called upon Eloise, but she hadn't answered the door. Either she hadn't been home or was avoiding the police. That, of course, had set my mind alight. If Eloise was avoiding the police, what could she possibly be hiding? And if she was home, why would she refuse to answer the door for Robert? Questions swirled in my mind, refusing to settle. Whatever the reason, Eloise needed to be interviewed. That much was clear.

The streets of London were abuzz with holiday cheer as I made my way to Eloise's flat. Snow dusted the rooftops, and the sound of carolers drifted through the air. It would have been charming if not for the dark cloud hanging over the Mistletoe Shoppe murder.

When I arrived at Eloise's building, I took a moment to steel myself. It was a modest place, with a narrow staircase leading up to the flats above a row of shops. Not the best of neighborhoods, but not the worst either. It was probably the best a shopgirl could afford. After climbing the stairs, I soon found myself at her door. I took a deep breath and knocked firmly.

Footsteps shuffled on the other side. Clearly, someone was home.

"Who is it?" a cautious female voice called out.

I could have chosen many names, but I decided upon the one she knew best. "Kitty Worthington," I replied brightly. "You might remember me from the shop, Eloise. I'm one of your regular customers. I was hoping to have a quick word with you."

There was a pause, long enough to make me wonder if she might retreat after all. Then, at last, the door creaked open a few inches, and Eloise peered out. She was a petite young woman with a nervous expression and hair the color of chestnuts tucked neatly beneath a woolen hat. The hat was odd but not unusual. It was rather cold.

"Miss Worthington? Is it really you?" she asked hesitantly.

"Yes," I said with an encouraging smile. "I promise I'm not here to trouble you, Eloise. I'd like to talk to you about the Mistletoe Shoppe and what happened to Mister Arkwright."

Eloise hesitated, glancing up and down the hallway before finally stepping back to let me in. Her flat was small but tidy, with a faint scent of lavender in the air. It was a bit cold inside. Thus, the reason for the hat. More than likely, she was trying to save money given her recent employment more than likely had come to an end. She gestured for me to take a seat on a worn but comfortable-looking armchair, and I obliged.

"I don't know much," she began, her voice trembling slightly. "I already told the police—"

"Who?" I interrupted gently.

"Inspector Bolton." She huffed. "He was not very nice."

With that I had to agree. Somehow Bolton had managed to talk to her after he'd taken over the case.

"I told him I hadn't seen anything." As she spoke, she glanced around the space avoiding looking me in the eye, a clear sign she was lying.

"That isn't quite true, is it?"

Her eyes widened, and I pressed on before she could deny it. "I understand why you might have been afraid to speak up, Eloise. It's a dreadful thing, what happened to Mister Arkwright. But if you saw anything that could help me find out who's responsible, it's important that you share it."

"You're not with the police?"

I shook my head. "I'm conducting my own private investigation."

"Why?"

"A friend of mine is implicated."

Her face filled with sympathy. "You're afraid he'll be charged with murder."

"Yes, I am. He's a good man, Eloise. He would never do such a thing. Please, won't you tell me what you saw?"

Eloise wrung her hands, her gaze darting to the window as though she might flee at any moment. At last, she let out a sigh and sank into the chair opposite me.

"I didn't mean to lie," she admitted. "I was scared, that's all. Mister Arkwright was always so kind to me. I didn't want anyone to think I had anything to do with what happened to him."

"I understand," I said gently. "But if you can tell me what you saw, I promise it will help."

Eloise took a shaky breath and nodded. "I went out for lunch that day," she began. "Mister Arkwright said it was quiet enough for me to step away for a bit. But when I came back, there was someone in the shop, arguing with him."

"Someone?" I hoped it hadn't been Hollingsworth. "Who?"

"I don't know her name," Eloise said, her brow furrowing. "I'd never seen her before. She was tall, with platinum blonde hair and a very sharp look about her. She was holding a piece of paper. A note she'd received. She seemed angry."

A woman! Thank heavens! The revelation sent a jolt of excitement through me. A mysterious woman, angry about a note she'd received, arguing with Arkwright on the very day he was killed. It was too significant to ignore. "Did she say what was in the note?"

Eloise shook her head. "I couldn't hear everything they were saying, but she kept pointing at the paper and raising her voice. She said something about it frightening her. She told Mister Arkwright to be careful."

"This woman," I said carefully, "Was she posh or—?"

"Oh, definitely posh!" Eloise rushed to say. "Why, she was wearing a fur coat that must have cost a bob or two. White one, too. Who goes around wearing a white fur coat as muddy as the streets are?"

A definite clue. "Maybe she arrived in an automobile. Did you notice one nearby?"

"Oh, there were lots, Miss. What with being the Christmas shopping season and all." She paused for a moment. "There was one thing that struck me as odd, though."

"What?"

"There was one stationed right in front of the shop. Other motorcars were honking at it. It took up so much space, there was barely any room to pass."

"Do you know what type it was?" Please let it be something easily recognized.

"A sedan, Miss. Black, long."

Well, that was no help.

"It had a hood ornament." She turned to me. "My sweetheart Bertie loves motorcars. He knows them all by heart."

Bless Bertie!

"What did the hood ornament look like?"

"A woman running with a circle beneath her feet. Bertie pointed one out to me before. He called it a speed nymph. A nymph is a woman."

"How clever of Bertie to know that!" A Bugatti. It had to be. Very few of those existed in London. Something I'd learned from Neville, the Worthington family chauffeur. "That's a wonderful clue, Eloise. It should help us with the murder investigation."

Her joy vanished in an instant. "Mister Arkwright was such a kind man. Why would anybody do that to him?"

"I don't know, Eloise, but I mean to find out. Did you see the woman leave?" I asked.

Eloise shook her head. "No, I didn't want to interrupt them, so I went around to the back door and waited for her to go. When I entered, Mister Arkwright seemed . . . unsettled. I asked if everything was all right, but he just waved me off and said it was nothing to worry about."

"But you worried anyway," I guessed.

"Of course I did," Eloise admitted. "It wasn't like him to be so curt. I thought about asking him again, but the shop got busy, and I didn't get the chance. And then . . ."

Her voice trailed off, and she looked down at her hands, which were clasped tightly in her lap.

"Eloise," I said gently, "you've been very brave to tell me this. I know it wasn't easy, but it might be exactly what we need to find out what happened."

Her eyes flicked up to meet mine, a glimmer of hope breaking through the fear. "Do you really think so?"

"I do," I assured her. "And I promise you, we'll get to the bottom of this. Now, what time did you leave the shop?"

"Five, Miss. Bertie and I were going to the cinema. So, Mister Arkwright allowed me to leave early."

I'd arrived barely a half hour after that. The murder could have only been committed in that half hour. "What will you do now that the shop is closed?"

She brightened up. "I'm getting married, Miss, in the spring. Bertie does not want me to work. He makes enough to support both of us. I'm moving in with my sister at the end of the month."

"Where does she live?" I casually asked.

She didn't hesitate to give me that address. A good thing. No matter where the investigation led, Eloise was a key witness. If I needed to talk to her again, I knew where she could be found.

As I left Eloise's flat, my mind raced with possibilities. Who was the mysterious woman? What delivery had sparked such a heated argument? Could she be Arkwright's murderer?

Salverton needed to know the information I learned from Eloise. So, I rushed home and put in a call to the number he'd given me from the telephone in my personal parlor. Given the sensitive nature of the enquiries at the Ladies of Distinction Detective Agency, I'd had a private line installed at home. Although I used it to make telephone calls, very few people knew the number—mainly those who worked at the agency, Robert, and now Lord Salverton. While I waited for him to telephone, I retrieved my journal and noted the new information. An hour later, I received a letter from Salverton noting a place and time to meet the next day. Not the method we'd agreed upon, but it was what it was. At the end of it, he'd written *Burn this.* I was just consigning the paper to the fire in the hearth, when Robert strolled in.

Drat!

CHAPTER 8

THE INVESTIGATION DEEPENS

"*D*arling," I said slightly nervous. "You're home early!" It was barely past two.

His brow wrinkled. "Is that a problem?"

"Of course not! I'm always happy to have you home." I barely stopped myself from clutching my hands. Robert was aces at reading body language. Doing so would be a clear sign of guilt.

His gaze narrowed. "What were you burning in the hearth?"

Any hope I had of him missing my action went up in smoke. Of course, he'd seen it. Better seek a diversion. Strolling over to him, I curled my arms around his neck and gave him a quick peck on the lips. "A love note from my admirer," I whispered against his lips.

He laughed. "Anyone I know?"

"Now, that would be telling!" I kissed him once more, this

time with more passion. "You are, and will always be, my own true love. No other man will ever measure up to you."

He shook his head and gazed lovingly at me.

Taking his hand, I drew him down to the sofa and accommodated myself next to him. "I've been thinking."

"Always a dangerous thing."

"Christmas is but a few days away—two to be exact. We will enjoy a Christmas feast—Cook has already planned it. But since neither my family nor yours can attend, I thought it would be a marvelous idea to invite Hollingsworth."

"It is marvelous, but he already turned me down."

I leaned away. "When did you invite him?"

"When I questioned him about the Arkwright murder."

"No wonder he refused. You issued the invitation while you were interrogating him." I brushed my thumb across the cleft on his chin. "I, on the other hand, will invite him as a friend."

"You believe you'll have more success than I did?"

"I know I will!"

He captured my hand and kissed the palm. "And how will you manage that, my love?"

"Through the judicial use of my womanly wiles." Leaning against him, I said, "I'll visit him tomorrow morning and then go shopping. I need to buy Boxing Day presents for our staff."

"I've already taken care of that."

"Where did you stash them?" I hadn't seen any gift-wrapped boxes. And I'd seriously searched.

"I didn't. I gift them cash every year. All I need do is stash pound notes in envelopes, write the staff's names across them, and distribute them." When I looked skeptical, he said, "I assure you, it's very much appreciated."

"I'm sure it is, darling, but I'd like to give them something more personal."

"Such as?"

"Well, Mister Black enjoys a very expensive Cuban tobacco which can only be found at one shop. Cook loves a particular gardenia scent. The maids adore fine lace handkerchiefs, and the footmen will appreciate fine leather wallets. I'm gifting Grace a pearl brooch. She'll be over the moon when she sees it. I'm stumped when it comes to Hudson, though." Robert's valet was an enigma. Always perfectly groomed, I had no idea what he enjoyed.

"Tickets to the theatre. He's never quite left his old life behind."

Hudson, a costumer at a theatre company, had come under suspicion in a murder investigation. After Robert cleared his name, he offered Hudson a position as his valet which Hudson readily accepted. His fashion sense was so acute, he could have opened his own bespoke shop on Savile Row. But catering to nobs, as he put it, was not in his nature. He much preferred the role of a gentleman's gentleman to Robert, the most admirable gent he'd met. "Should we get him a subscription at The Majestic? That way he can choose which plays he'd like to attend."

Robert cupped my cheek. "He will very much appreciate that."

We spent the rest of the day discussing both everyday matters and Christmas. After supper, I shared with him the letter I'd received from Mother. They'd settled into Wynchcombe Castle, and had participated in a couple of holiday activities. Margaret was fine. Sebastian was trying to hover as little as possible, with not much success. They'd heard about the Arkwright murder. Everyone was concerned Hollingsworth had been implicated, especially Mellie. Well, that made sense. She was his sister after all.

"When I write back to Mother should I share what we know?" I asked Robert.

"Best not. Given Bolton is now in charge of the investigation, we have no idea what he's discovered."

"You're right. I just wish we could do more."

He sighed. "So do I."

~

THE FOLLOWING morning dawned bright and clear. With no snow in the forecast, it was a perfect day to go shopping for the Boxing Day gifts. But first I had to visit Hollingsworth.

Rather than drive my own roadster, I had a footman hail a taxicab. It took no time for me to arrive at Hollingsworth's townhome. He'd inherited it from his father who'd lived in it more than the family's country seat. The former marquis had only married to satisfy the need for an heir. His mother had found the perfect candidate in Hollingsworth's French mother. Once Hollingsworth was born, he returned to London to resume his gambling and carousing lifestyle. He only returned to his wife's bed after Hollingsworth became deathly ill. Fearing his heir would die, he resumed marital relations. Months later, Mellie was born. By that time, Hollingsworth had regained his health, so his father returned to London and once more took up his dissolute ways. No one in his family mourned when he passed on to his glory.

When Hollingsworth's butler opened the door, I rushed to say, "I'd like to see Lord Hollingsworth on a personal matter." I wanted to make it clear I was not there to investigate.

"Of course, Lady Robert." He bowed and opened the door wide. "Please come in."

After he showed me to the drawing room, it took no time for Hollingsworth to make an appearance.

"My dear Kitty, how wonderful to see you." Taking my hands, he kissed both of my cheeks.

Immaculately dressed and, thankfully, sober, he was once more the Hollingsworth I knew and loved.

"Would you like some coffee?" he asked. He knew I preferred that beverage over tea.

"Yes, thank you."

Turning back to his butler, Hollingsworth requested the service.

"How is Lord Rutledge?" he asked taking a seat on a chair across from me.

"No change."

"Ahhh. Robert is taking it hard."

"Yes, he is. I'm here to invite you to Christmas supper."

"How very kind of you. Please accept my regret."

"No. I will not accept it, Hollingsworth."

"But—"

"Don't say you are otherwise occupied. I know you're not. First of all, you did not travel to Wynchcombe Castle with my family and your own sister. Why? I have no idea. And no one of any worth has invited you to Christmas supper."

"And how would you know that?"

"Practically everyone has departed the city for their country estates. Very few members of high society are left. Those who know Robert and I haven't left town assume you are spending it with us."

"I may wish to spend Christmas alone."

"If you think I'll let you spend the entire day getting drunk, you have another think coming. I. Will not. Allow it."

"You don't know everything, Kitty. I may have a lady friend I wish to spend the day with."

"You don't have a lady friend, Hollingsworth. The sea is your mistress, remember?"

"I do not wish to discuss the Arkwright murder."

"I promise to avoid the topic on Christmas Day."

Having dismissed all his objections, he finally conceded

defeat. Before I left, I got him to agree he would join us for Christmas supper.

～

My next appointment was the one Salverton had arranged. Once more ensconced in a taxicab, I headed in the direction he'd provided. The address led me to a modest but well-kept townhouse on a quiet street. The sharp contrast between this unassuming neighborhood and Salverton's was startling. But then it made sense. You wouldn't want to locate a safe house among the homes of the elite. The afternoon sky hung low and gray, casting a muted glow over the streets of London as I stepped out of the motorcar and onto the narrow pavement.

Taking a fortifying breath, I lifted the heavy brass knocker shaped like a lion's head and gave three sharp raps. Moments later, the door creaked open to reveal a tall man with a somber face and neatly combed hair. His appearance was formal but devoid of grandeur—much like a butler, but not quite. Somewhere underneath that facade, an intelligence agent lurked.

"Good afternoon. Your name, please." His voice was measured but polite.

"Lady Marigold. I believe Bunny is expecting me." The code name Salverton had given me.

"Indeed. This way, if you please."

He stepped aside, and I entered a narrow hall with polished wood floors and sparse furnishings. The air carried a faint scent of leather-bound books and pipe smoke. I followed him down the corridor until he opened a door, revealing a study bathed in the soft glow of a desk lamp. Salverton rose from behind a mahogany desk, his expression grave but welcoming.

"Lady Marigold," he greeted me, extending his hand. "Thank you for coming." Once the man at the door left, he said, "I trust you've come with news?"

"I have." I took the chair he indicated by the fire. "I spoke with Eloise, the assistant at the Mistletoe Shoppe. Her information was ... illuminating."

Salverton leaned forward, his interest evident. "Go on."

"She mentioned a woman who seemed oddly out of place —elegant, well-dressed, and far too polished to be browsing Christmas trinkets in such a modest establishment. She said the woman had a haughty air about her. She was tall, blonde, and possessing a commanding presence. Eloise overheard an argument between the shopkeeper and the woman who apparently was holding a sheet of paper and appeared to be warning him."

Salverton's brows knitted as he considered this. "Did Eloise provide anything further—such as a name?"

I shook my head. "No name. But she did mention the type of car parked in front of the shop—a Bugatti. Not exactly common in London, particularly among women."

"A Bugatti. Now that's interesting." Salverton stood and walked to the window, staring out at the quiet street below as if weighing his next words. When he finally turned back to me, his eyes were sharp with recognition.

"During the Great War, a certain circle of financiers operated behind the scenes, brokering deals that kept their fortunes intact while others suffered. One of the key figures in those arrangements was Lord Denton, a senior member of the House of Lords. His wife, Lady Denton fits the description you've provided."

A chill prickled at the back of my neck. "Lady Denton? You're certain?"

Salverton nodded gravely. "She's quite a beautiful woman, much younger than her husband. She was not from the upper class, far from it. But she managed to snare him. You can imagine how she managed that. Within a year, she wrangled a marriage proposal from him." Salverton shrugged. "Nothing like an old fool I suppose. If she's involved, this could be much larger than we imagined. And that Bugatti . . . I'll confirm whether she owns one, though I suspect she does."

"Thank you," I replied, struggling to contain the swell of apprehension. "Lady Denton's involvement raises troubling questions. What is her connection to the Mistletoe Shoppe? Obviously, she knew Mister Arkwright well enough to argue with him. Was she involved in her husband's deals during the Great War?"

"She came into his life after the deals had been brokered. We never discovered what role she may have played in those. One thing we knew, she traveled quite extensively with him prior to and after the marriage. Supposedly, Lord Denton couldn't bear to be parted from her."

"No fool like an old food indeed," I said.

Salverton offered a tight nod. "I advise caution. If the woman in the shop was indeed Lady Denton, she is quite ruthless. She will not hesitate to protect her husband's interests—by any means necessary."

I met his gaze and felt the weight of his warning settle on my shoulders. "I understand."

"Leave the matter of the Bugatti to me," Salverton added. "In the meantime, I suggest you avoid drawing unnecessary attention to yourself. You've already come dangerously close."

The notion of sitting idle while he gathered information didn't sit well with me, but I nodded, nonetheless. "Of course."

Salverton saw me to the door, his parting words lingering in my mind as I stepped outside. The crisp air was a bracing reminder of the reality I now faced. I hailed a taxi and instructed the driver to take me to Harrods. If I was to remain inconspicuous, I might as well spend the afternoon in a suitably festive fashion.

∼

THE GRAND ENTRANCE to Harrods glistened with holiday cheer, its windows a dazzling display of crimson bows, frosted pine boughs, and golden fairy lights. Inside, the air was warm and fragrant with the scent of pine and cinnamon. I made my way through the bustling aisles, selecting small but thoughtful gifts for our household staff.

While gliding through Harrods' galleries—pausing to admire embroidered gloves, silk shawls, and sets of fine porcelain teacups—a movement at the edge of my vision caught my attention. A statuesque woman in a white fur-trimmed coat swept past, her platinum-blonde hair gleaming under the store's chandeliers. My breath caught. She matched Eloise's description precisely. I felt the blood rush to my cheeks at the sight of her. After all, what were the odds I should encounter her in that precise moment, given everything Eloise had told me?

I tried to dismiss it as coincidence—that a wealthy lady might shop at Harrods this close to Christmas was hardly unimaginable. But my instincts refused to be mollified. I sensed, even from that distance that the woman was Lady Denton and furthermore did not wish to be recognized. The way she tensed, the quick glances over her shoulder . . . it all seemed rather clandestine. I lingered by a display of gloves, surreptitiously watching her. Soon enough, she paid for something—a hat, I think—and then swept out of Harrods as though fleeing a scene.

As a peculiar urgency gripped me, something compelled

me to follow her. After all, if Lady Denton had indeed been near Arkwright around the time of his death, I could not let her slip away with her secrets. Once outside, she strode to the curb, where a gleaming Bugatti awaited her, a chauffeur at the wheel. I watched in stunned silence as she stepped inside, and the engine purred to life.

With heart pounding, I waved at a taxi and asked the driver—in as calm a manner as possible—to follow Lady Denton's motorcar at a discreet distance. The driver's eyes lit up with intrigue as he merged into the flow of traffic.

My heart hammered the entire ride, the streets of London passing in a blur of motor vehicles and the swirl of post-holiday crowds. Ignorant it was being followed, the Bugatti weaved deftly through the streets, its sleek form a blur of black and silver. The chase led us from the bustling avenues of Knightsbridge to an affluent part of town. Finally, the Bugatti slowed and turned onto a familiar street. I gasped aloud when I recognized the address. As I watched her ascend the steps, cloak swirling about her ankles, she cast furtive glances over her shoulder before disappearing inside. Lady Denton had just entered the address I'd visited just this morning—Hollingsworth's home.

CHAPTER 9

HOME AGAIN

I swept into the front hall of my home, my cheeks still tingling from the cold outside and my mind swirling with the morning's revelations. Slipping out of my gloves, coat, and hat, I handed them to Mister Black, who hovered discreetly near the entrance. The weight of all I had learned pressed upon me like an invisible cloak. I could scarcely decide which thread of concern to pull first.

Thankfully Robert was not home which left me free to pace the floor of my personal parlor replaying the day's events in my mind. Was the woman in the Bugatti Lady Denton? Or had I chased a shadow? No. It had to be her. It would be too much of a coincidence that she was visiting Hollingsworth. And that begged the question. What business could she possibly have with him? The thought sent a chill down my spine, far colder than the winter air.

So many questions rattled in my head like marbles in a tin box. Were Lady Denton and Hollingsworth in league with each other, or were they adversaries? Was she there to confront him, or perhaps to confide in him? The uncertainty gnawed at me.

Having missed my luncheon, I requested coffee service, though I was far from certain I could stomach even a biscuit. My nerves were taut—every sense on edge from the events of the day. As I paced, I allowed my thoughts to circle back to the conversation I'd had that morning with Salverton. I had shared Eloise's most recent statements: how she had seen Lady Denton at the marionette shop around the time poor Mister Arkwright was murdered. It was scandalous, to be sure. Lady Denton, the picture of refined aristocracy, lurking about a humble toymaker's establishment on that particular, tragic day. The moment I recounted Eloise's words, I could see on Salverton's face how very grave he believed the matter to be.

With so many wild imaginings rolling around my head, I needed to jot down my thoughts. Only when I reached for my journal did I realize dusk had begun to fall. As I lit my desk lamp, I heard a muffled conversation and the sound of the front door closing. Robert had arrived. My journal would have to wait.

When he entered my parlor, it took but one look to realize something was very wrong. Fearing the worst, I asked, "Your brother? Has something . . . ?" I couldn't even finish what I meant to say.

"Not him. No."

"Something else then?"

He raked an exasperated hand through his dark hair. "Bolton came to see me this afternoon."

My stomach twisted. "What did he say?"

"He's gathered enough evidence to arrest Hollingsworth for Arkwright's murder."

A dreadful pause descended, broken only by the faint crackling of the hearth. "Surely not. On what basis?"

Robert's gaze hardened. "They found footprints at Arkwright's shop that match Hollingsworth's boots, or so Bolton claims. They discovered his fingerprints as well."

"That doesn't prove anything. Hollingsworth's been there before. His fingerprints would be at the shop."

"That doesn't explain the marionette with his name carved into it."

"Somebody clearly is trying to put the blame on him. Arkwright surely wouldn't have had time to do it himself."

"That's just it. He probably had the time. The poison was not a quick-acting one. It would have taken twenty minutes or so for him to die. Time enough to carve Hollingsworth's name on a marionette when he realized he was dying. But the most damning evidence is Bolton found a witness who saw Hollingsworth at the shop shortly before the murder took place."

My heart pounded uncomfortably. Bolton's case sounded damning at first glance, but I refused to accept the conclusion. Steeling myself for what was to come, I took a deep breath. "I have reason to believe that the actual culprit might be someone else entirely."

Robert threw me a sharp look. "Who might that be?"

I swallowed, forcing myself to speak calmly. "Eloise—Arkwright's shop girl—told me she saw Arkwright alive after Hollingsworth would have left. She also said that she saw a woman who I believe to be the wife of a peer arguing with Arkwright. If Eloise is right, that means Hollingsworth could not have committed the murder."

Robert's jaw slackened in surprise. "How do you know all this?"

"I visited Eloise's flat yesterday." I shared with Robert everything Eloise had said. "When she returned from lunch, she saw Arkwright arguing with a woman, platinum blonde hair, dressed in a white fur coat."

"You think this woman is the wife of a peer?"

"Yes."

"How do you know?"

Now came the hard part. "I can't tell you."

His brow furrowed. "Can't or won't?"

"Can't."

He turned around and offered a few choice expletives to the wall before swiveling back to glare at me. "Salverton."

I did not say a word.

He took several slow, measured steps toward the parlor door. But before he could close it, a maid and a footman arrived with the coffee service I'd requested. After quickly setting it up, they rushed out as if all the hounds of hell were on their heels. Clearly, they'd heard him.

"Would you like some coffee?" I asked offering him a cup.

"No!" More hair raking.

Settling on the settee with the coffee and a biscuit, I waited for him to regain his equilibrium. It wouldn't take long. Robert's outbursts were rare. And when they occurred, it took little time for him to become his usual self.

After a few minutes of pacing, he turned to me. In a much calmer tone, he asked, "When you spoke to Eloise, did she tell you Arkwright was still alive after Hollingsworth departed?"

"No. That's not what she said. That's what I deduced."

"Please explain."

"Arkwright allowed her to leave at five—which was early for her—so she could attend the cinema with her sweetheart, Bertie. I arrived around half past five to find Arkwright dead. The murderer, whoever, he or she was would have had to poison him during that half-hour's time. Arkwright's body was still warm when I touched him which means he probably died no more than a few minutes before I arrived."

"That doesn't mean Hollingsworth didn't do it. It could have been him as much as anyone else."

"No. It wasn't."

"How do you know that?"

"You, being a man, probably don't realize it. But Hollingsworth wears a very specific fragrance that reminds me of the sea," I replied, meeting his eyes. "I did not note that scent. What I did note were pine and an exotic scent—patchouli and vanilla."

He waved a hand in the air, dismissing my conclusion. "Candles, more than likely."

"The Mistletoe Shoppe does not sell candles or anything that transmits scent. The pine came from the garlands hanging around the shop. The exotic fragrance could have only come from the last person who was there before me. Arkwright's killer more than likely."

He blew out a breath. "It won't do any good. Bolton won't accept that as evidence, and, frankly, neither would I."

"I know that. But it does indicate Hollingsworth wasn't the last person there. He may have been at the shop, but he was not the last. Maybe the witness saw him while Eloise was out to lunch."

"Eloise did not see Hollingsworth?"

"No."

"But she did see the woman?"

"Yes. She left, but she could have returned."

"You need to talk to Eloise again. Ask her if she saw Hollingsworth or anyone else lurking about when she left for the cinema."

I understood why that was up to me. He couldn't get involved. Not with Bolton heading up the investigation. "I will. Tomorrow." I patted the space to my right. "Come have a biscuit. They're quite festive. Cook has outdone herself." She'd decorated them with snowmen and Christmas wreaths and trees. Once he'd eaten one, I said, "Hollingsworth will be joining us for Christmas supper."

"He agreed?"

"Yes. I promised him we wouldn't talk about the investigation. We will make believe it doesn't exist."

His gaze softened as he folded me into his arms. "Whatever would I do without you?"

"Turn into a grumpy old man."

He laughed and kissed me. "Right you are."

CHAPTER 10

CHRISTMAS DAY

I awoke on Christmas morning with an effervescent sense of joy stirring in my breast. Despite the chill of winter pressing against the windows, there was a brightness to the day that gave it a certain magic.

"Happy Christmas, darling," Robert curled an arm around me and urged me closer to him.

I turned toward him and whispered the same against his lips. "Our first together."

He kissed me softly, gently. "May there be many more."

I curled my hand around his bristled cheek. "Indeed."

Having slept later than we should, we rushed through our morning routine. Otherwise, we would not make the Christmas service on time. Something devoutly to be avoided. As we readied ourselves, we chose our warmest formal attire. The roads were bound to be busy filled with others bound for churches and family gatherings. For a moment I indulged in a moment of sadness as I recalled previous years when the Worthington family set out together. But I quickly shook it off. Robert was my family now. One I dearly loved. I would see my parents and siblings soon enough.

The journey proved uneventful, and I stared out the Rolls Royce window at the frost-laden homes. They shimmered under the pale morning sun like a patchwork quilt of diamonds. As Robert carefully maneuvered the motorcar, he squeezed my hand gently, smiling at me. In that moment, I felt we were blessed indeed to share such a splendid morning together.

Upon arriving at the church, we found the entire edifice draped in holly and ivy. A large wreath adorned the massive double doors, and the crisp scent of evergreen greeted us the moment we crossed the threshold. Families that had come from near and far gathered in the pews, greeting one another and sharing tidings of gladness. The choir began with a softly sung hymn, building toward triumphant crescendos, and I closed my eyes to let the music wash over me. Christmas truly was a day of hope and renewal, reminding us all of the blessings we might otherwise overlook in our daily routines.

After the service concluded, Robert and I exchanged brief words with the vicar and some acquaintances before making our way back to our motorcar. The wind had picked up and was now busy swirling snow through the air. The drive home felt longer than the drive there, perhaps due to the promise of the Christmas present exchange waiting for us. I couldn't wait to open our gifts in our cozy library amid the quiet comfort of the room, surrounded by the faint aroma of old books and the gentle crackle of the fireplace.

Entering our Eaton Square townhome gave me a profound sense of being exactly where I belonged. The staff had lit fires in all the main rooms, and the enticing smell of roasting goose and spiced puddings wafted in from the kitchen.

"Happy Christmas, Mister Black," I said to our butler while unbuttoning my coat.

"Happy Christmas, Lord and Lady Robert," he replied.

Once we finished handing him our outer garments, Robert and I walked hand in hand toward the library. I sighed at how wonderful it all was. The polished mahogany shelves glistened in the amber glow of the newly stoked fire.

"What a perfect Christmas this is," I murmured, tilting my face up to Robert's for a kiss.

He didn't disappoint. As he brushed his lips against mine, he said, "It's not too much of a disappointment, is it? Not being able to spend Christmas with your family, I mean." A frown creased his brow.

I curled my arms around his middle "I miss them, yes, but you are my family now, Robert. I will see them soon enough."

Together, we settled by the hearth, eager to exchange our gifts. I found myself fidgeting with excitement, anticipating the moment Robert would open the present I had chosen for him.

We had barely settled onto the plush sofa, with parcels in our laps, when the telephone in the hallway rang. I sighed, glancing at Robert, who wore a playful expression of mock exasperation. "I'll get it," he offered gallantly, setting his package aside.

It didn't take him long to return. "It's your mother," he said.

"Oh!" I jumped from the sofa and rushed toward the telephone located in a tiny alcove outside the library. I picked up the telephone and held the receiver to my ear. "Happy Christmas, Mother," I greeted, hoping the warmth in my voice conveyed how glad I was to hear from her.

"Happy Christmas, my darling Kitty," Mother replied. The

crackle of the line indicated she was calling from quite a distance. "I do hope you and Robert are well and enjoying the day."

"We are," I assured her. "And you? How is everyone?"

There was a brief pause on the other end of the line, followed by my mother's gentle laugh. "We are well, though we have had a bit of a surprise in terms of weather. A snowstorm is expected in two days' time, so we've decided to cut short our stay at Wynchcombe. We'll be taking the train to London tomorrow."

Delight surged through me. I would see Mother, Father, my siblings, and close friends sooner than anticipated. "Tomorrow!" I exclaimed. "That is wonderful news indeed. I have missed you."

"I know you have, dearest. Margaret and Sebastian will remain at Wynchcombe Castle for another week or so. But the rest of us shall arrive hopefully before noon. Weather permitting, of course. We hope to travel while the railway lines are still passable."

"I'm sure they will be, Mother." She'd never been a fan of traveling by train. The moment the word snow had been mentioned, she must have immediately made plans to return.

I caught Robert's questioning gaze and whispered they were returning early. Smiling, he nodded he understood. "Safe travels. Call as soon as you're back home."

"I shall. One more thing, Kitty. We discussed holding a small gathering for New Year's Eve at Worthington House. Just the family and a few friends. That doesn't interfere with your plans, does it?"

"We have none," I responded without hesitation. "It will be lovely to ring in the New Year with our nearest and dearest."

"Excellent. Well, I won't keep you any longer. Enjoy the rest of your Christmas Day. Give my love to Robert."

After promising to do so, I ended the call.

Robert raised an eyebrow. "Well?"

I relayed the news that the Worthingtons were returning tomorrow, though Margaret and Sebastian would not be among them. And that Mother would be hosting a New Year's Eve gathering.

Robert smiled warmly. "I'm glad. You'll be happy to see your family again."

As we resumed our seat on the sofa to open our gifts, my heart felt delightfully light, as if a burden had lifted. As I peeled back the wrapping on Robert's gift to me, I found a gorgeous leather-bound journal, its cover embossed with golden fleur-de-lis designs. The pages, when I flipped them, were edged in gold as well. It was exquisite, and I couldn't resist pressing it to my chest. "Thank you. It's beautiful."

"Read the inscription," Robert said.

"To Catherine, the love of my life. A journal to record the times of our lives."

"Oh, Robert." My eyes misted as a lump grew in my throat. After wiping away the tears, I said, "I'll need more than one, you know."

"Not to worry. There will be one for every year." He retrieved a gayly wrapped package from his pocket and handed it to me.

"Another one?"

"You don't think I'd give you only one."

By the shape of the box—a large square—I could tell it was jewelry. Sure enough, it was a velvet-covered jewelry case. I flipped it open to reveal a parure set made up of a diamond and emerald necklace with a pair of matching earrings and a bracelet. I was so stunned I couldn't say a word.

"Do you like it?"

"Like it? It's stunning, Robert. Where? How?"

"They're part of the Rutledge collection. No lady has worn them for over a hundred years. I had them all cleaned for you." His gaze was a question. "It's not too much, is it?"

I curled my hand around his cheek. "No, my darling, it's not. I shall wear them with pride." I looked up at him through my eyelashes. "Of course, you only wear something as beautiful as this to special occasions."

"The theatre or the ballet?"

"Ummm, I was thinking about something more intimate."

"Our bed while you're wearing nothing else."

"You read my mind, Inspector."

He spent the next few minutes styling the jewelry around my neck, my ears, and my wrists while covering me with kisses, in some rather outrageous spots. Finally, when he had me breathless on the sofa, I said, "You have yet to open my present to you, my darling."

"Ummm, we'll resume this later."

I tossed him a saucy grin.

He was rather speechless when he opened my present. I had managed to secure a rare edition of one of his favorite historical volumes, one that had come highly recommended by a mutual friend in the antiquarian book trade. He turned it over in his hands, gently tracing the raised lettering along the spine. The genuine pleasure in his gaze filled me with such happiness that I hardly noticed the chill of the winter day seeping through the windows.

My second gift to him was a pair of pyjamas, something he never wore to bed. For a second he appeared confused and then he recalled that one night at Rutledge Castle when I'd joked about it. Getting into the spirit of the thing, he said, "I shall wear them tonight."

"Don't you dare! I prefer you very much unclothed."

Eventually, we had to stop our tomfoolery to prepare ourselves for Christmas supper. The table would be set with the best china, the silver polished to a perfect shine, the candelabras draped in garlands of greenery, and the center of the table boasting an elaborate arrangement of poinsettias.

Rather than have my maid Grace and his valet Hudson help us with our garments, Robert and I opted to assist each other. He helped me with my festive gown—a deep forest green velvet with intricate lace along the sleeves and neckline. I fussed with my hair, pinning it back with pearl-studded combs. He'd managed to slip into a snowy white shirt but required my aid with his evening jacket.

Just as I was slipping on my shoes, we heard a firm knock at the front door. Moments later, someone rapped on our bedchamber door. "Lord Hollingsworth has arrived, Lord Robert."

A gentle flutter went through me, for I had half expected him to send his regrets. But he'd kept his promise to join us for Christmas supper. I recalled the serious conversation we had shared regarding our ongoing investigation. Today, however, I intended to keep my promise. I would avoid any talk of mysteries, conspiracies, or troubling matters. Surely, on Christmas Day, we could enjoy a respite from intrigue.

Robert and I descended to the main hall, where Hollingsworth was shaking off the snow from his coat. His mahogany hair was dusted with white flakes, and there was a rosy flush to his cheeks. He looked up at us, his aquamarine eyes shining with good cheer. "Happy Christmas," he greeted warmly. "I've brought gifts," he added, lifting a basket which held ribbon-wrapped packages.

"Happy Christmas, Hollingsworth." I offered my cheek for a kiss and Robert shook his hand.

We drifted into the drawing room where we accepted mugs of steaming mulled wine from Mister Black. The scents of oranges, cloves, and cinnamon drifted up, enticing me to take a quick sip. After Hollingsworth handed us his gifts, I unwrapped mine—a lovely silver key charm, intricately wrought with swirling designs, intended to be worn on a chain.

"For unlocking secrets," he said with a crooked grin, and then, catching my eye, he raised a cautionary brow. "But not tonight."

I laughed, grateful for the gift and for his lighthearted approach. Robert, for his part, received a small hand-tooled leather folio with compartments for carrying important papers. It was perfectly practical for a detective inspector who often had many documents to manage for each case. The thoughtfulness behind such gestures warmed me, and I was reminded yet again how dear Hollingsworth had become to both of us.

I handed him the gifts I'd chosen for him—a book of poems and tales about the sea, including *The Rime of the Ancient Mariner* and *Annabel Lee*. Our second gift was a gold compass. On the card attached to it, I'd written, "So you may always find your way home."

When he lifted his gaze, I spied tears. But Hollingsworth being Hollingsworth quickly turned it into a jest.

We headed to the dining room, where the table gleamed beneath the soft glow of candles. The servants had outdone themselves with the feast: roast goose stuffed with herbs and apples, braised vegetables, sweet puddings, and a mince pie that made my mouth water just from its aroma. We took our seats and engaged in the usual chatter of the holiday, exchanging anecdotes about our families and the memories of Christmases past.

I was tempted to refer to the investigation, but I quickly quelled the urge. More than once, I'd sensed Hollingsworth's subtle glance at me, as though to say, "Not now." And so, we kept to lighter topics. The conversation, underlain with genuine affection, rolled smoothly along. By the time we reached dessert, my heart felt full—of good food, contentment, and gratitude that this Christmas Day had been filled with such magic.

After supper, we withdrew to the drawing room once more, where the staff had prepared a tray of spiced tea and dainty cakes—though heaven knew we had eaten more than enough already. Yet it was traditional to finish with tea or coffee, so we indulged ourselves. For a while, we talked of music and traveling. Hollingsworth regaled us with a humorous tale of an ill-fated trip he had taken in his youth, which ended with him sleeping in a stable after missing his connection. His recounting had us laughing so hard that my sides began to ache.

It was nearing midnight when I finally admitted defeat to my own drowsiness. "I believe I shall retire," I told the gentlemen, who were engaged in a spirited debate about the merits of brandy versus port after a large meal. I smiled, sliding my hand along Robert's shoulder. "You two enjoy your port, or your brandy, whichever it may be." It might be the last chance they would have for some time to sit in peace together.

Robert's gaze held mine for a moment—tender, understanding, and appreciative all at once. He knew I was offering him time with his closest friend, something I wholeheartedly supported. Turning to Hollingsworth, I added, "Please stay the night. It is snowing again, and the roads will be perilous."

Hollingsworth nodded, for indeed the wind had picked up significantly. "Thank you. I believe I shall. I'd rather not risk my neck tonight."

Content that I'd looked after their comfort, I bade both men goodnight and made my way up to our bedchamber. There, I changed into a soft, warm nightgown, the plush rug beneath my feet soothing my tired soles. I could still hear their laughter echoing faintly in the halls as I turned down the covers. In my mind's eye, I pictured Robert pouring a final glass of port, the firelight dancing across the polished table, while Hollingsworth lounged in an armchair, continuing his good-natured banter. There was something deeply satisfying about knowing my husband could share this camaraderie—especially in times so fraught with secrets and shadows.

CHAPTER 11

THE MORNING AFTER

I awoke the following morning to a soft blanket of silence. Robert had already risen. But before he'd left me, he'd whispered "Good morning," and dropped a kiss on my lips. Pushing aside the bedclothes, I slipped into my dressing gown and crossed to the window. My breath caught as I beheld a perfect winter wonderland: heavy snow draped across the gardens and lawns, branches bowed under the weight of fluffy white piles, and the sky a vivid hue of pale grey that heralded more snow to come.

Dressing quickly in a thick woolen gown, I made my way downstairs. The house was bright with the reflection of the morning light on the snow, giving every polished surface an extra gleam. I found Robert and Hollingsworth in the dining room, their plates laden with a hearty meal of eggs, bacon, and toast. The aroma of fresh coffee greeted me, making me realize how hungry I was after the previous night's revelry.

"Good morning, gentlemen," I said cheerfully, taking my

seat. A footman poured coffee for me, and I cupped my hands around its comforting warmth. Robert leaned over and kissed me on the cheek, murmuring a soft greeting.

Hollingsworth, still looking somewhat sleep-ruffled but good-natured, offered me a courteous nod. "Sleep well, Kitty?" he asked.

"Like a log," I replied, lifting my cup. "And you?"

He smiled wryly. "Your guest room is too comfortable, I fear. I may never want to leave."

Robert chuckled. "You're welcome as long as you wish, my friend. At least until you must brave the roads again."

I glanced out the window at the gentle swirl of flakes. "From the look of it, I imagine anyone traveling throughout London will have quite the adventure." After a worried thought, I said, "I just hope my family finds their way home without too much trouble."

Robert squeezed my hand. "They will. Neville is an experienced chauffeur."

"Yes, there is that." But the Worthington motorcar could only accommodate my family. The others would need to take a taxi unless Ned had arranged for other reliable transportation. As efficient as he was, he probably had.

A restless tension suddenly tugged at me. I'd promised not to broach the subject on Christmas Day, but that vow had expired with the stroke of midnight. We were now well into the morning of the twenty-sixth. The weight of unanswered questions bore down on me as my mind buzzed with possibilities. Hollingsworth, I was certain, possessed some of the missing pieces—if he didn't have the complete picture, at least he had something of value.

I tried to steady my racing thoughts, absently tearing off a corner of toast. It tasted like stale worry on my tongue. Across the table, Hollingsworth's gaze flicked to me—warning me. I could sense his silent plea not to dig up these secrets so soon after the holiday. But my curiosity burned hotter than my caution.

Clearing my throat, I spoke softly, although a hint of steel tinged my voice. "Hollingsworth, I need to ask you about the lady who visited you yesterday in the early afternoon."

With a controlled deliberateness, he set down his fork, the resulting clink loud in the hush. His eyebrows lifted, a silent reprimand. "Kitty," he said, with mild reproach, "you promised."

My heart quickened at his gentle chastisement, but I lifted my chin anyway, defiance curling around me like a protective cloak. "I promised to avoid the subject on Christmas Day. That day is over. I must know what she wanted."

Robert, who had been casting uncertain glances between us, finally spoke. "Is this the wife of a peer you mentioned?"

"Yes." My tone was clipped, betraying the frustration simmering beneath.

Hollingsworth narrowed his eyes. "And how do you know that?"

Before I could answer, the dining room door burst open, startling me so thoroughly I nearly dropped my toast. Mister Black came rushing in behind the figure who had the audacity to stride in unannounced.

"I beg your pardon, Lord and Lady Robert," Mister Black panted. "He rushed past me—I couldn't stop him." His outraged glare fell upon our intruder: Lord Salverton.

I exchanged a look with Robert, noting the tension stretched taut across his features. Whatever this was, it was clearly urgent. "It's all right, Mister Black," I said, trying to school my voice into calm as my heart banged against my ribs. I noticed the grave set of Salverton's mouth. This was not a conversation meant for other ears. "I'd like all the staff to leave, please. We need the space to ourselves."

Mister Black bowed stiffly, a flicker of concern in his

eyes. "Of course, milady." He beckoned the footmen out, and, in seconds, we were alone with the man who had so abruptly invaded our breakfast.

Summoning what remained of my composure, I drew a steadying breath. "Lord Salverton, you look as if you have important news. Would you care for something to drink? Coffee? Tea?"

He gave a curt nod, the tension in his shoulders palpable. "Coffee would be welcome. Thank you."

While I poured him a cup, Robert and Hollingsworth exchanged apprehensive glances. No one spoke until Salverton had settled in a chair, hands wrapped around the steaming mug. Then we silently braced ourselves for whatever he had to say.

"Lady Denton has fled the country." His words fell like a hammer blow.

Hollingsworth sucked in a sharp breath. I clutched the edge of the table, a sudden jolt of foreboding rippling through my chest. "Why?" I asked, though an uneasy sense of the answer already twisted my stomach.

"Presumably because she was about to be assassinated."

My insides turned cold. Robert set his jaw, a muscle jumping there. "What are you talking about?" he demanded through clenched teeth.

Salverton's gaze slid from me to Robert. "I suppose there's no point trying to keep you out of this discussion."

Robert's voice was as frigid as the winter wind outside. "None whatsoever. You asked Catherine—my wife—to investigate a matter fraught with danger. You dragged her into something that could threaten her life. I have every right to know what's going on."

A fleeting flicker of regret crossed Salverton's features as he inclined his head. "Very well." He took a measured sip of coffee, as if bracing himself. "This all began during the Great War."

He paused, and a weighty hush filled the air. I could feel my heart in my throat. Hollingsworth, rigid with tension, kept his gaze trained on Salverton, ready to parse every word.

Salverton continued, "Exchange of information. Our intelligence agents gathered it in Germany, passed it to France, who relayed it to us. The same was done in reverse. After the war ended, we dismantled much of our courier network. We believed there was no further need."

Robert nodded, his eyes shadowed with understanding. "But things changed," he said.

"Yes," Salverton replied grimly. "Some Germans never stopped their work. Certain industrialists foresee Germany rising again. They're designing advanced weaponry for when the time comes."

I pressed a hand to my throat, trying to quell the roiling dread. "Didn't the Treaty of Versailles prohibit them from that sort of thing?"

Salverton gave a mirthless smile. "Prohibition doesn't stop everyone, Lady Robert." He shifted. "In any event, Lady Denton was a go-between—her husband's interests in France intersected with those of British intelligence."

My breath caught. "She was one of our spies?"

"Agents," he corrected. "Yes."

A wave of shock and admiration warred within me. My mind reeled with the implications. "But you made her sound like she was working for Germany."

"I couldn't trust you, not entirely," Salverton said flatly. "Her life was in danger. I had to safeguard her identity."

Robert's brows knitted, anger flaring anew. "Is that why Arkwright was killed?"

"We believe so, yes."

"But why?" My voice came out shakier than I intended.

Salverton's somber gaze landed on me. "Arkwright received intelligence through toy deliveries—little packets were hidden within. This was done by British agents, but we've discovered there was a traitor among them. One of our own fed pieces of information to the Germans. A double agent. We never discovered who it was."

I felt a shiver roll through me, like a frigid draft snaking across the floor. "And now that person is 'cleaning house,' getting rid of anyone who knows them?"

Salverton inclined his head, silently confirming my worst fear. "That's what we believe. Arkwright was the first. Lady Denton would have been the second."

"But how would Lady Denton know other couriers? Wouldn't they operate in secret?"

"Supposedly, yes. But not always. Sometimes, they were required to work in pairs."

"And Hollingsworth?" I glanced at my old friend, stomach tight with concern.

"He was one of the couriers."

Hollingsworth exhaled slowly. "My mother was French. I was fluent, so I was recruited to carry toys from France to England and deliver them to Arkwright or take them from him."

Each word dripped with regret, as though he wished he'd never accepted such assignments. "Did you know other couriers? Besides Lady Denton?"

"A couple."

Salverton's eyes were unreadable. "Since Hollingsworth was a courier, that places him in the suspect pool."

"But he wouldn't kill Arkwright!" I said vehemently, my voice trembling with indignation.

Salverton lifted a pacifying hand. "I know that, Lady Robert."

"You must share the names of all the couriers with Bolton, so he can investigate them."

"He can't do that, Kitty," Hollingsworth said.

"He's right," Salverton said, a note of regret in his voice. "Couriers' names are classified. To protect them. To protect the entire network."

The unfairness of it all—of letting Hollingsworth's life hang in the balance—made the back of my eyes burn. "So you'll let them charge him if he can't prove his innocence?"

Salverton's lips thinned. "We must protect our agents, even if some of them are suspected of wrongdoing. We cannot risk exposing everyone."

Heat flooded my chest, an anger born of fear for Hollingsworth. "Then we must find the real killer," I said, gripping my hands until my knuckles whitened. "Who else served as couriers? Surely you can share that much with us."

Salverton pressed his mouth into a hard line. "I can't."

My frustration rose, making my breath come short. "Surely you don't expect us to stand by and watch Hollingsworth become the next victim—or the next accused. If you won't help, we'll do it ourselves."

Robert reached across to cover my hand, adding the comfort of his touch to my determination. Hollingsworth sat rigidly, caught in the crosshairs of a shadowy game. And amidst it all, Salverton simply watched, that neutral calm of his revealing nothing—and promising danger.

"You're on your own. I can no longer provide you with any information or assistance. But if you come close to compromising state secrets, be assured action will be taken that you will regret."

With that, he came to his feet and left.

CHAPTER 12

A NEW DIRECTION

*A*fter Salverton's abrupt departure, we opted to continue our discussion in the library. But before doing so, Robert and I gathered our staff in the drawing room and presented them with their Boxing Day presents. Smiles and pleased grins abounded as one and all, they thanked us for our generosity. Mister Black had apparently been chosen to deliver a warm, heartfelt speech which Robert and I truly appreciated. Robert dismissed them for the rest of the day, joking we would somehow muddle through without them. Cook, more than likely afraid we'd set the house on fire, reminded us there'd be no need to light the cooker as there was plenty of food in the icebox. As they took their leave, they shared their plans for the rest of the day with us. While some chose to venture out, most decided they'd just retire to their rooms to enjoy a well-earned rest.

Once the last one filed out of the drawing room, Robert and I walked hand in hand toward the library where

Hollingsworth awaited us. With the staff either gone or retreated to their rooms on the top floor, the house felt unusually silent—the sort of breathless hush that followed in the wake of startling news.

The moment I stepped into the library, I inhaled the familiar perfume of old leather and rejoiced in the warmth of the crackling fire. It was a comfort, this space. Yet right now, it intermingled with the dread tightening around my chest.

Hollingsworth had made himself at home on the leather sofa and helped himself to a tot of whiskey. A little early in the day, but I wasn't about to mention it. It might very well be the last chance he'd have to enjoy such a thing.

Robert closed the door behind us before turning around. "Well," he said, his voice hushed, "it's been quite a morning."

Hollingsworth raised his glass. "Pour yourself some whiskey. It will make you feel better."

"I think I will," Robert said heading toward the cabinet where the crystal decanter was located. "Would you like one, darling?"

He meant the question for me, but, of course, Hollingsworth couldn't help himself. "I believe I'll have some more, sweetheart." He held out his glass.

Robert shook his head and poured two fingers worth of whiskey into it. "Catherine?"

"None for me, thank you."

I sank onto the settee and let out a long, shaky sigh. A swirl of questions churned inside my mind. If I closed my eyes, I could nearly see them dancing in the dark—a chaotic waltz with no clear pattern. "Salverton gave us so much. And yet so little," I whispered.

Hollingsworth nodded. "I suppose we should be grateful for what we learned from him." His voice sounded distant, as though he were speaking from the far side of a cavern. "Lady Denton fled to save her life. Salverton was clear about that."

"Why did she come to see you?"

"To warn me that my life was in danger. She had done the same with Arkwright. She hinted at what she intended to do, though she didn't come right out with it."

"What about her husband? Will he search for her?"

"I doubt it. He's grown quite senile since the Great War."

"But how will she live? She'll no longer be able to afford her lifestyle, I imagine."

"I wouldn't feel too sorry for her. Denton was quite generous with her. Showered her with many gifts, mostly jewelry. She'll be able to lead a comfortable existence from the proceeds of the stones alone, I imagine. If she's smart, and she is, she'll keep a low profile."

"Where do you think she's gone?"

"Somewhere warm. She hated our English weather."

While Hollingsworth and I talked, Robert crossed to the fireplace and prodded at the low flames to coax them higher. He was always the calm in the storm. But there was a tightness in his jaw that told me he was as unnerved as I was. "Did she not confide anything else in you when she visited?" he asked, glancing over his shoulder at his friend.

Resting the glass on the small table in front of him, Hollingsworth gazed at his hands. "Not in so many words," he began, shoulders slumping as he remembered. "She arrived unannounced and told me I was in danger. When I asked her how she came by this knowledge, she merely alluded to the fact that certain 'friends' in her circle had warned her that the noose was closing. If Arkwright was dead, then we could be next. She advised me to leave the country as well."

Anger—and something resembling heartbreak—flickered in his eyes. "But how could I? I won't leave my sister behind, and she's too stubborn to flee with me. Besides," he added, swallowing hard, "I'm not a coward. If someone is framing me for murder, or trying to pick us off one by one, I would much rather face it head-on. I can't even conceive of sneaking off under cover of darkness and leaving you all behind."

My heart twisted painfully at his words. I felt a sudden urge to reach out, to pat his hand, to soothe the tension in his shoulders. But Hollingsworth wasn't the type to be comforted by such gestures. He was an independent man—fiercely so—and I knew that offering him sympathy might only stir his frustration further.

"We wouldn't want you to run," I said softly, leaning forward in my seat. "But as it stands, there is something else pressing: Bolton." His name came out on a bitter exhale. "He's certain to arrest you for Arkwright's murder. He's probably merely biding his time until he gathers enough for a warrant. A single rumor, a stray piece of evidence, might be all it takes."

Hollingsworth nodded, grim acceptance in his eyes. "Yes. I've sensed his suspicion since the first day I encountered him. To be frank, I'm surprised he hasn't already put me behind bars."

Robert set the fireplace poker aside and crossed to me. He placed a hand lightly on my shoulder, as though he was presenting a united front. "We won't let that happen without a fight," he said. "If we can only figure out who the other couriers are—someone else must have knowledge that could exonerate you."

Hollingsworth spread his fingers on the armrest, glancing between Robert and me. "I didn't know the others by name. That's how it was, you understand. Everyone's identity was compartmentalized. We were each simply cogs in a larger wheel of intelligence. But . . ." His gaze grew thoughtful, lips compressed as though trying to recall something from the recesses of his memory. "Once, during a handoff, I spotted a figure slipping away after meeting someone in a café. I recognized his face—though he wasn't a man of rank. He was a valet, I believe. Later, I came to learn that he might be in the service of Lord Peterson."

"Lord Peterson," I repeated. I had never met him, not directly, but I knew he was a friend of Lord Denton's, a gentleman with a reputation for traveling extensively during the war. "You think his valet could have been a courier?"

Hollingsworth shrugged. "It's only a suspicion. But it makes sense. Lord Peterson was close to Lord Denton. If Lady Denton was a courier, it seems likely that there might be interconnections."

"Yes," I agreed, feeling a burst of cautious optimism. "We should investigate it. Anyone else?"

"I only heard about her. Never saw her. She went by the code name "Nightingale"." He laughed to himself. "We all had one."

"What was yours?"

"Hook."

"As in Captain Hook from *Peter Pan?*"

"Yes. It seemed amusing at the time."

"So, we have this Nightingale and Lord Peterson's valet. We should start with him. Find out his name at the very least. Perhaps something will arise from that lead."

A smile, fleeting and grim, crossed Hollingsworth's lips. "Perhaps." It was almost like he'd given up hope. Well, I wouldn't let him.

My heart fluttered with purpose. I had felt like a leaf caught in a gust of wind, whipped this way and that by the uncertainty swirling around Arkwright's murder and Lady Denton's disappearance. Now, we had an inkling of a direction, a slender thread to pull. It was better than sitting by, wringing our hands in silent dread.

"Eloise might be able to help us as well," I said. "She spent so much time at The Mistletoe Shoppe—she may remember seeing someone who didn't quite fit in. Or perhaps she noticed recurring visitors who did not purchase any toys. It's a long shot, but we need to find out."

Robert nodded. "Yes, precisely. The more lines of inquiry we have, the better chance we can catch the real culprit out." His dark eyes flicked to Hollingsworth with concern. "And keep you safe."

Hollingsworth made a sound somewhere between a chuckle and a sigh. "Safe. I'm not sure that word has meant much to me lately. But I appreciate it."

The quiet fell among us, thick with unspoken thoughts. None of us said it outright, but we were all thinking it: every moment we delayed might bring Bolton one step closer to slapping irons on Hollingsworth. Every bit of progress in our investigation needed to be swift if we were to avoid that terrible scenario.

Eventually, I rose from the settee and moved to the window, drawing back the heavy brocade curtain. The afternoon sunlight lay across Eaton Square, gilding the edges of the garden in a deceptive calm. It reminded me that outside these walls, life continued at its usual pace—motorcars rattling over cobblestones, children laughing in parks, families celebrating the second day of Christmas. Our private crisis was just that: private and urgent and terrifying.

"We've done all the planning we can for now," I said at length, turning back to my husband and Hollingsworth. "We should allow our minds a little rest—just a short reprieve—before we overwork ourselves into uselessness."

Hollingsworth gave a reluctant nod, as though he dreaded stepping away from the immediate problem. But Robert reached over and squeezed his arm lightly. "A respite. It's best. Fresh eyes can do wonders."

As if on cue, there was a quick rap on the door, followed

by James, the footman who'd volunteered to remain on duty in exchange for an entire day off. I immediately braced, fearing more dire news. "Yes?" I asked, my voice taut.

"Begging your pardon, my lady," James said, "but the telephone rang just now. Mrs. Worthington."

"I'll take it. If you'll excuse me." Once again, I picked up the telephone and put the receiver to my ear. "Mother. You're home?"

"Yes, my dear. We were surprised by all the London snow, but we're happily settled into Worthington House once more."

"So happy you made it without too much trouble."

"So am I," Mother said with a soft sigh. "See you soon?"

"Yes, of course. As soon as it can be arranged."

"Until then." And with that, she ended the call.

Returning to the library, I closed the door behind me. While I was talking to Mother, a thought had occurred to me.

"Is everything well?" Robert asked.

"Yes. They're back. That means Ned is as well."

"You thought of something," Robert said.

I nodded. "Ned was in the War Department during the Great War. He might very well have insight or at least some contacts who can open doors for us. That could be invaluable."

Robert pursed his lips. "He'll be bound by the Official Secrets Act, as all three of us are. He won't be able to give you explicit information."

"But he could guide us," I insisted, my heart leaping with renewed hope. "Give us hints, direction—he might know what questions to ask, which offices in Whitehall to approach, or which lines of enquiry are dead ends. That alone would be immeasurable."

Robert and Hollingsworth exchanged a glance, each seeming to weigh the possibilities, before they both nodded.

"It's worth a shot," Robert said.

A swelling warmth filled my chest as I saw their guarded expressions ease with cautious optimism.

"I'll call him tomorrow morning. Ask him to join us here at two. It'll be like old times."

"The Investigative Committee, you mean?" Hollingsworth asked, a small smile curving his lips.

"Yes." I couldn't help but return his smile, though there was a tightness in my chest that refused to fully relent. At least we had a plan now.

Hollingsworth rose and offered a small bow of gratitude. "Thank you." His gaze landed on me with sincere warmth. "I'm grateful, Kitty. To both of you. Without your determination, I'd feel truly alone in all this."

I swallowed the sudden rush of emotion. "You will never be alone, Hollingsworth," I said. "Robert and I will always stand by your side.

We parted ways shortly thereafter with the promise of meeting again the next day. Robert and I busied ourselves with making sure the library was returned to rights. Never let it be said we were slackers. Yet while carrying the glasses to the kitchen to be washed, my mind never truly left the swirling questions of our investigation.

At odd moments—while raiding the icebox for our dinner and undressing for the night—I found my thoughts drifting back to the revelations of the morning. I would picture Lady Denton, fleeing the country in desperate haste, and feel a pang of sympathy. I could almost see her anxiously looking over her shoulder, scanning the horizon for any sign of pursuit. And Arkwright—poor Arkwright, who would never again greet us at The Mistletoe Shoppe with a polite tip of his hat and a gentle word. Anger mixed with sorrow.

It felt like an eternity, but in reality, we would only have to wait until the next day to speak with Ned. However, life had a way of lobbing new uncertainties into the mix. Very early the following morning, we were roused by a knock on our bedchamber door. Robert and I both rose in a hurry and pulled on dressing gowns. Heart lurching with unease I wondered who would call at this hour. It was barely eight.

Mister Black as it turned out. Looking unusually distressed, he stood in the corridor outside our bedroom door. His demeanor spoke volumes before he even said a word. My stomach twisted as he bowed curtly and whispered, "Lady Robert, Lord Robert, there is . . . there is news."

"News?" I repeated, dread creeping over me.

"From a constable with a message from Scotland Yard," he said. "They've arrested Lord Hollingsworth. Inspector Bolton personally placed him under arrest for the murder of Mister Arkwright."

CHAPTER 13

DISASTER STRIKES

I glanced back at Robert, whose face had gone pale. There was a moment of stunned silence between us. My hands were trembling so fiercely I had to clench them into fists to still them.

When at last Robert regained his composure, he spoke in a voice that tried to be calm but quivered at the edges. "Thank you, Mister Black. Please have the Rolls brought around. I shall be leaving shortly."

"Of course, Lord Robert," Mister Black said, dipping his head in that dignified manner he never seemed to lose, then left us alone.

I slowly let out the breath caught in my lungs as I gazed at Robert. My mind struggled to piece everything together. So, Bolton had finally made his move. Had he found another piece of evidence? Or was this a bluff—an attempt to pressure Hollingsworth into confessing or revealing what Bolton believed to be a secret?

Robert's gaze rested on my face, concern etched into every line. "Catherine," he murmured, gathering me into his arms. "We will handle this."

I clutched my dressing gown, struggling to keep an even tone. "We had so little time . . . We've discovered so little! I—I can't bear the thought of him sitting in a cell, charged with a murder we know he didn't commit."

"I'll go to Scotland Yard at once, find out where they've taken him. As soon as I do, I'll speak to him." There was a hard edge to Robert's voice I rarely heard.

I raised a resolute gaze at him. "He'll need a solicitor. I'll contact Sir Frederick Stone." The barrister who'd represented Robert when he'd been charged with murder in Oxford.

Robert nodded, the lines on his brow easing. "Yes. We can post bail if we're allowed. Bolton can't detain him without legitimate evidence."

Well, he had that. But was it enough? My mouth went dry as I pictured Bolton twisting facts to suit his narrative. "I'll telephone Ned as well," I said, determined to do my part. "Let him know the state of things. I'll ask him to join us this afternoon. We should have made some progress by then."

At that, Robert offered me the faintest hint of a smile. "Absolutely. We need everyone on board. We'll make sure the truth prevails."

My heart still pounded wildly as we rushed to dress. Under any other circumstances, we would have ignored propriety altogether, but Hudson and Grace stood guard with comb and brush at the ready, looking scandalized at the notion of us rushing out disheveled. Despite the urgency, I couldn't help a weak smile at their fussing.

"You must present a proper appearance at Scotland Yard, Lord Robert," Hudson insisted. "Otherwise, you will not be taken seriously."

He had a point, though it felt like a nuisance in such a dire situation. Finally, with only the bare minimum achieved—Robert hadn't even shaved—we hurried downstairs.

A fraught energy clung to the house. Mister Black waited in the foyer, his eyes reflecting the tension we all felt. Yet he spoke in a level tone. "James has brought the Rolls around, milord. It awaits you outside."

"Thank you, Mister Black," Robert said. Then he turned to me, his fingertips barely brushing my cheek, a fleeting promise that we'd see this through. "I'll call as soon as I have any news."

"Please," I whispered. "I hope to have some of my own by then."

He gave my hand one last reassuring squeeze before he pulled on his coat and gloves. With a swift nod, he strode out the door, the weight of our worries trailing after him.

"Anything I can do for you, milady?" Mister Black asked gently.

I mustered a grateful smile. "Yes, please arrange for coffee in my personal parlor."

He inclined his head. "Certainly. Shall I also have the staff bring you some breakfast?"

My stomach churned at the thought of food. "Yes, thank you," I managed although I doubted I could eat.

As he relayed my request to a footman, I stood in the hallway, pressing my palms to my flushed cheeks. I had to be strong for Hollingsworth—for Robert—and for myself.

With my thoughts buzzing, I hurried to my parlor. The next order of business would be to contact Sir Frederick Stone. For that, I would need my private telephone. I doubted he would be in his office. I just prayed somebody was. Indeed, that turned out to be the case. There was a law clerk on duty. After I explained the situation to him all I could do was wait for Sir Frederick's return call. Since it would take some time to reach him, I decided to telephone Mother and find out if Ned was there.

Mother was not a fan of the telephone, indeed any modern contraption. But when our butler relayed I was calling, she picked it up soon enough. "Kitty? Anything wrong?"

"Unfortunately." I explained what had happened and asked if Ned was there.

"He is, although he's just about to leave for the office."

"I need to talk to him."

"Of course, dear. Let me know if there's anything I can do."

"I will. Thank you, Mother."

One of the maids gently knocked on the parlor room door. After I yelled "Enter" she proceeded to lay out the coffee service on the parlor's small round table. I didn't have time to pour a cup before Ned came on the line.

I explained as succinctly as I could what had happened. "I want to convene the investigative committee this afternoon at two here at Eaton Square. Robert and I would like you to attend. Can you make it?"

Not for one second did he hesitate. "Of course."

"Thank you, Ned."

The line had barely clicked into silence when it trilled again, jolting my already frayed nerves. "Yes?" I answered, holding my breath.

"Miss Worthington—pardon me, Lady Robert, I should say. Frederick Stone here."

My shoulders sagged in relief. "Thank you for calling me back, Sir Frederick." My words tumbled out in a rush as I described the arrest, the possible prejudice of Bolton, the looming threat of scandal, and—worse—the possibility of Hollingsworth rotting in a cell.

"That is indeed serious," came Sir Frederick's measured reply.

"He's innocent!" I exclaimed.

"Of course he is. I doubt Lord Hollingsworth would stoop to poisoning. If he intended to kill someone, he would more than likely use a blade."

Despite the tension crushing my chest, I had to smile at his dry humor.

"There is a matter of national security involved," I added, lowering my voice. "I can't go into details."

He let out a thoughtful hum. "That certainly complicates matters, but it won't deter me. I'm happy to represent Lord Hollingsworth. But first I need to speak with him. Do you know where he's being held?"

"Not yet. Robert is at Scotland Yard finding out as we speak. As soon as he knows, I'll have him call you."

"Excellent," Sir Frederick said, giving me his direct number. "I'll be waiting."

"Thank you," I whispered, my grip tightening on the mouthpiece. "I know Hollingsworth will be in good hands."

After the call ended, I sank back against the wall, my head resting on the paneled surface. With each action we took, I felt a flicker of hope. Bolton wouldn't prevail if we kept our wits about us. We would not allow Hollingsworth's good name—and his future—to be destroyed.

I poured myself a cup of the now lukewarm coffee and forced myself to eat the cold eggs and toast. I would need my strength to get through the day. No sooner had I finished eating, when the telephone buzzed.

"Robert?" It had to be him.

"Hello, Catherine."

"Did you find Hollingsworth?"

"I did. Bolton is holding him here at Scotland Yard until his case comes up before the magistrate which more than likely will be tomorrow. If the magistrate finds sufficient evidence to charge him with murder, he will be sent to Pentonville Prison. Did you talk to Sir Frederick?"

"I did. He wants you to call him with Hollingsworth's location. He's willing to represent Hollingsworth, but he needs to talk to him first."

"Naturally."

After I gave Robert the number, he ended the call before I had the opportunity to tell him I'd talked to Ned. His nerves were on edge, much as mine were.

Having done as much as I could, I turned my focus to the upcoming investigative committee meeting. It might only be Ned and me, but I intended to share as much as I could with him. But first I had to alert Mister Black. At the very least we would need coffee and sandwiches as the meeting might last a while. Once I'd done that, I settled down to jot down everything that I knew. It seemed like only a few minutes had elapsed before there was a knock on my parlor door.

Mister Black, as dignified as ever, stood in the corridor. "Your guests have arrived, milady. Per your instructions, I've shown them to the library."

Guests? Who could they be? I was only expecting Ned. Well, there was only one way to find out.

I walked into the library to find not only Ned but Richard, Mellie, Emma, and Marlowe.

Her eyes shining with merriment, Emma walked toward me and kissed both of my cheeks. "We hear we have a new intrigue to investigate. How fun!"

CHAPTER 14

THE INVESTIGATIVE COMMITTEE MEETS

I was so surprised I didn't know what to say.

Ned did, though. "I tried to keep them from coming," he said while everyone accommodated themselves around the library.

Emma laughed. "He did, not that it did any good." She'd settled on one of the settees where Marlowe quickly joined her.

"Ollie's my brother," Mellie said, her eyes sparkling with emotion. "I have a right to be a part of this." Frankly, I'd felt the same emotion when Ned had been suspected of murder.

"Is there a drop of whiskey in the house?" Marlowe asked. "I'm going to need some fortification to proceed."

"You didn't have to come, Marlowe." Emma showed no sign of rancor toward him. She was only making a point.

"Where thou goest, so will I, my sweet." Marlowe curled his hand around hers and brought it to his lips.

Emma accepted the gesture with a smile.

Seemingly, we would not be subjected to fireworks from them. Thank heaven! I didn't think my nerves could take them.

I clasped my hands as I studied them. It wasn't the first time we'd gathered to investigate a murder. Except for Richard, that is. He'd been away in Egypt for the last several years. Ned, my ever-supportive brother; Richard, newly returned to the family; Emma, my brilliant partner at the Ladies of Distinction Detective Agency; Lord Marlowe, Emma's suitor, with a penchant for trouble; and Mellie, Hollingsworth's sister, whose eyes shone with equal measures of determination and fear.

Sadly, I had to present them with the stark reality of this enquiry. "I thank you all for volunteering to help with the investigation. But for some of you that will not be possible."

"Why not?" Mellie challenged. She must have realized she'd be one of those kept out of the loop.

"For reasons of national security," Robert said strolling into the library.

I turned to face him. "Darling, I didn't hear you arrive."

He curled an arm around me and dropped a kiss on my head. "No wonder with all the chattering going on." Taking in our friends and family, he offered them a smile.

"What does Arkwright's murder have to do with national security?" Emma asked.

I folded my hands in front of me. "That we cannot explain. I'm sorry. Emma, Mellie, Marlowe. I thank you, but you must leave."

"No," Mellie refused. "There must be something we can do."

"May I make a suggestion?" Ned asked.

"Yes, of course."

"Bifurcate the investigation. Those of us who have clearance to handle national security matters will handle those enquiries. Marlowe, Emma, and Mellie can investigate those that don't."

I turned to Robert and whispered, "What do you think?"

"We're treading on thin enough ice as it is." He gazed around the library at our friends. "But there might be something they could do that would not involve national security."

In the end, we decided to go along with Ned's suggestion. We temporarily banished Emma, Marlowe, and Mellie to the drawing room, while we shared the confidential facts of the investigation with Ned and Richard, both of whom had signed the Official Secrets Act. Ned, because of his work for the War Department. Richard, for the missions he'd undertaken during the Great War. We never knew what they were. But given his facility with languages, we imagined at least a few involved infiltrating Germany.

"Thank you again for volunteering to help. But first, I must ask. Richard, are you up to this? You've only just recuperated from your bout of malaria. Are you fit enough to handle this enquiry?"

Richard blew out a breath. "I wish everyone would stop mollycoddling me. I assure you I can handle whatever comes."

Even so, I would ensure the tasks assigned to him would not involve strenuous physical activity. "Fine. Let us get started then."

Between Robert and I, we shared the basic facts of the murder and the damning evidence against Hollingsworth.

"So, he denied going to the shop that day?" Ned asked.

"Yes. But Inspector Bolton has a witness who saw him there," Robert replied.

"Who?"

"Bolton did not share that information with me. I imagine it will be presented at the hearing before the magistrate. Sir

Frederick Stone has agreed to represent Hollingsworth. He will relay to us the witness's name."

"We'll need to verify the witness is telling the truth," I said.

"Absolutely," Robert said, pouring himself some whiskey. Neither Ned nor Richard accepted his offer of the same. They'd already chosen the strong coffee that one of our maids had served.

"We'll also need to find out who else visited the shop that afternoon between five and half past five," I said. "Eloise, the shop girl, left at five to attend the cinema with her sweetheart, and I arrived at half past five. So that means the murder could have only been committed during that half hour."

"Not necessarily," Richard said.

"What do you mean?" I asked.

"You said they found traces of the poison in a teacup."

"Yes."

"What if someone gave him a tin of tea as a gift and he only opened it that day?"

"I didn't think of that," I said. "That means—"

"—The tea could have been given to Arkwright at another time," Robert finished. "That would make it much harder to identify the murderer."

"Was the poison in fact in a tea tin?" I asked him.

"I was not made privy to that information, Bolton was."

"You need to find out, Robert. Through your acquaintance in forensics maybe?"

"I will. Leave it to me."

"I'll add it to the list of questions to ask Eloise. She may have witnessed someone giving Arkwright a tin of tea as a present. And she would know his tea habits."

"So, how do you want us to proceed?"

"Well, I will visit Eloise. Robert will return to Scotland Yard and see what he can learn from forensics."

"I'll also attend the hearing before the magistrate," Robert said. "That's to be held tomorrow morning. Bolton will need to present all the evidence he's gathered against Hollingsworth at that time."

"The more information we have the better," I said.

"I can visit the Explorers Club," Richard suddenly chimed in. "I don't know how many members will be there. But there might be a few in attendance, eager to get away from the hustle and bustle of the holidays."

"And how would that help?"

"While on . . . assignment during the Great War, I ran into a couple of chaps I knew to be members of the Explorers Club. Sometimes they played more than one role."

"Were they couriers as well?" I asked.

"Whatever King and Country required, Kitty."

"Exactly so," Ned agreed.

"If they're not at the club, I can obtain their details from the membership roster. Hopefully, they haven't fled to their country estates. If they are in fact in London, I could drop in for a chat, find out if they knew other couriers."

"That all sounds perfectly marvelous, Richard. Thank you."

"Thank you, Kitty. This . . . assignment will make me feel useful again."

Poor old bean. That's all he really wanted. Once this investigation ended, we would need to find something useful for him to do. It would make a difference in his world.

"What about you, Ned?" I asked. "Do you have any ideas?"

"You mentioned Lord Peterson. Or rather Hollingsworth mentioned him."

"That's right."

"He's a client of Worthington & Son." The investment firm Father owned. He'd made Ned a full partner a couple of years ago. "I can request a meeting to review his portfolio. With the new year, there are several opportunities to explore."

"Brilliant! But how would it get you to his valet?"

"As a soon-to-be-married chap to the daughter of a duke, I'm sure to be rubbing elbows with high-ranking peers, maybe even royals themselves. My manservant, while adequate with business attire, is not up to the task with more formal wear. Maybe his valet has someone he could recommend?"

I burst out with laughter. "You make it sound so logical. Would he believe you?"

"Lord Peterson is easily flattered. Once I mention how well turned out he always is, he will readily agree to introduce me to his valet."

"Hopefully, you can obtain some useful information from him." I glanced at Robert. "That's the four of us assigned to tasks. Do you have anything else you think we should explore?"

"Not at the moment. We shall just have to see what develops."

"Shall we bring the others back in?"

He nodded.

Once Emma, Marlowe, and Mellie rejoined us, Robert and I shared what we could with them.

"I think we should visit the crime scene," Emma suggested. "We need to see what you saw. Sans the dead body, of course."

"Can that be arranged?" I asked Robert.

"I believe so. With Hollingsworth's arrest, no one is guarding the shop."

"Do that in the morning then. Say ten o'clock?" I suggested.

"That's awfully early," Marlowe said.

"You can always stay home," Emma suggested.

"I'll have to make the sacrifice," Marlowe replied. "Don't expect me to be at my best, though."

Rising from his seat, Richard approached me. "Does he always complain that much?" he whispered when he reached me.

"It's all a game to him. Believe it or not, he's quite brilliant at deduction."

"If you say so." After pouring himself more coffee, he returned to his spot next to Ned.

"We'll take a close look at the shop and see if anything stands out," Emma said.

"Do you have another assignment for us?" Mellie asked. Clearly, she was eager to do more than inspect the toy shop.

"We have several avenues of enquiry we're working on. Let us see what develops."

"We could question the other shop owners after we've finished our examination," Marlowe suggested. "Maybe one of them noticed something unusual."

"Excellent idea."

"Shall I bring my motorcar around to Worthington House in the morning?" Marlowe asked.

"Best take a taxicab. You don't want to call attention to your automobile." I glanced at my watch. It was nearing five. "I believe that's enough for today. We'll reconvene tomorrow. Would two provide us with enough time?"

"Make it three," Richard suggested. "I don't know who I'll find at the club."

"Very well. Three it is. If you get held up, please telephone."

Ned jumped to his feet. "Speaking of which, I need to make the arrangements we discussed."

Richard joined him. "And I'll start with my task."

"At this hour?"

"Best time to find who I need to find."

Within a few minutes, we found ourselves devoid of our guests.

"What about you?" I asked Robert. "Do you intend to leave as well?"

"No. Nothing I can do until morning. I'll need to have an early start, though."

I curled my arm around him. "Then let's make the most of tonight."

"Anything special?"

"Supper in our bedroom and then let's see where the night takes us."

"You read my mind."

CHAPTER 15

CLUES AND FINDINGS

Although I was eager to make my way to Eloise's flat the next morning, I forced myself to wait until ten to leave home. It would be beyond rude to arrive at an unseemly hour. After climbing into the taxicab one of the footmen had hailed for me, I pulled out my journal to read over my notes. Thankfully, there was little traffic, probably due to the holidays, so the driver delivered me swiftly to Eloise's address. As I'd done before, I climbed the narrow staircase and softly knocked on her door. I prayed she was home. For all I knew, she'd already moved to her sister's house.

But I needed not worry. She was indeed within. "Who is it?" she cried out.

"Kitty Worthington." I hadn't come empty-handed as I'd asked Cook to box some scones and pastries for her.

In the next instant, the door swung open. Eloise stood on the other side. Whereas before she'd been neatly attired and groomed, today was a different story. Her curls were an untamed tumble of ringlets as though each strand had a mind of its own. Her dress was dulled by a coat of grime, tracing its path along the bodice and settling into the folds of the skirt. Despite her disarray, there was a spirited glow in her eyes. "Miss Worthington. I wasn't expecting you. Please excuse the mess," she said pointing to the space behind her.

Boxes of varying sizes stood in precarious stacks against the walls. The place smelled of dust and cardboard, indicating a thorough packing.

"Nothing to be excused. I know what it's like to prepare for a move." Of course, I'd had the staff do most of it before my things were transported to Robert's townhouse before our wedding day. Still, I understood. "May I come in?"

"Please."

She opened the door wider for me, and I walked through.

Stepping around a half-packed crate of dishes, she said, "Bertie, my sweetheart, he said it's best if I don't stay here on my own. After what happened to Mister Arkwright . . ." She swallowed hard, tears springing briefly to her eyes. "So does my sister for that matter. With all the news in the dailies about the murder, they're afraid for me. But the man's been caught, hasn't he? That's what I read in the papers."

"They've apprehended a suspect, yes. But I think they got it wrong." I offered her the box of pastries. "I've brought you treats to thank you for your assistance."

"Oh, ta, Miss." She blushed. "And me without a plate." She pointed to the crate. "I've boxed them all up."

"You can eat them from the box. Needs must and all that."

"Maybe later. Please sit, Miss Worthington." She pointed to the one empty chair before placing the box on a spot on the kitchenette counter. "Did you have more questions?"

"As a matter of fact, I do." I flipped open my journal where I'd jotted the questions I wished to ask her. "Do you recall if Mister Arkwright had any visitors or acquaintances in the days before . . . ?" I allowed the rest of the question to hang in the air. No sense mentioning what she already knew.

"Yes, well. Let me see if I can. Everything was such a muddle. We were quite busy what with Christmas practically upon us. And we had parcels arriving practically every day. It was my responsibility to open them, you see. Mister Arkwright would price them, and I would arrange them on the shelves."

"I can imagine how busy you must have been."

After she took some time to think, she said, "Actually, come of think of it, there were two—a lady and a gentleman. They came the same day."

"Were they together?"

"No. They arrived separately."

"Could you describe them?"

"The first visitor was a very lovely lady, dark-haired and quite . . ." She hesitated, trying to choose her words delicately. "Buxom," she finished with a blush. "Wearing a stylish burgundy hat with black trim and a black stole. She looked, oh, I don't know—like a cinema star."

"What about the gentleman?" I asked after writing down the woman's description.

Eloise's brow furrowed in thought. "A fussbudget of a man: short, precise in his speech, and so particular about where he placed his gloves and cane. Very smartly dressed, with a neatly trimmed mustache. You could almost smell the pomade in his hair."

"That's a wonderful description, Eloise. Did you hear what they discussed with Mister Arkwright?"

"No, I was busy with the customers in the store. They both gave him wrapped gifts, though. That much I noticed."

"Do you know what they were?"

"No. Like I said, the shop was busy. Although . . ."

"Yes?" I prompted her.

"Well, later I spotted a tin in the back of the shop. A tea tin. When I wondered about it, Mister Arkwright mumbled something about a gift."

"Did he say who gave it to him?"

"No. But it had to be from the lady or the gent. I hadn't seen it before."

"Do you recall precisely when the visitors were there?"

"The day before Mister Arkwright . . ."

"I understand," I said writing that down as well. "Did the gentleman provide a name?"

"No, nor did she," Eloise said apologetically. "They both came in, chatted with Mr. Arkwright for a bit, and then left."

"And they both brought gifts?" She'd already answered the question, but I wanted her answer to fix in her mind.

"Yes. The lady's was a pretty little parcel. I didn't see what was inside, but it was wrapped in gold paper with a red ribbon. The man's was a small box. It was tucked under his arm."

"Did you find out what they were?"

"No. But later that day, Mister Arkwright pointed out the tea tin—he said it was from India. The design on the outside was so colorful. Ornate patterns, bright saffron, and turquoise details, if I remember right."

I was almost certain that was where the poison had been found. I would have to ask Robert.

"Was that the first time you saw it?" I asked gently, resting my pen on the page.

She nodded. "Yes. Absolutely. It was so distinctive you see. To my knowledge, he never opened it. I certainly never brewed any tea from it."

A twinge of excitement rippled through me. The possibility that the poison had come from that tin loomed larger with every word. "So, you saw it for the first time after both visitors had come and gone?"

"Yes, that's exactly right."

I pressed a hand to my chin. "He didn't say who had given it to him?"

She frowned. "No. I assumed it was the fussbudget man, because, well, a woman might have given something more personal, like those sweets he sometimes received from admirers. Mister Arkwright was a rather genial man. Then again, the lady could have just as easily gifted it. I truly don't know."

Exhaling slowly, I snapped shut my journal. "Thank you. This is very helpful. Eloise, please—if anything else comes to mind about that day, write it down and get word to me." I handed her my business card.

"The Ladies of Distinction Detective Agency, Hanover Square," she read. "Coo, Miss. A real lady detective."

"That's right. That's what I am." I glanced at the boxes piled everywhere. "When do you depart for your sister's house?"

"In two or three days, depending on when Bertie can get away," she replied, her voice softening as she looked around her flat. "I hate to leave this place, but it's for the best."

Giving her a comforting smile, I rose from the chair. "Things will sort themselves out, Eloise. Thank you for your time. I hope to get to the bottom of this quickly."

She walked me to the door. "You will let me know what you find."

Pressing her hands, I said, "I will."

"Good luck, Miss Worthington," Eloise said with quiet sincerity as I stepped out, then closed and locked the door behind me.

Indeed, I would take all the luck I could. We would certainly need it.

CHAPTER 16

TROUBLING THOUGHTS

After hailing a taxi, I pressed my shaking fingers to my temple, trying to steady myself. Despite my swirling thoughts, I opened my notebook and reread the notes I'd hastily scribbled at Eloise's:

Two visitors; dark-haired woman—gift; fussbudget man—gift; new tea tin from India.

Each word glared up at me like an accusation. That tin from India—it had to be the source of the poison. If we could prove it, then Hollingsworth's nightmare might end. My pulse thrummed with equal parts dread and determination. We had no choice but to uncover the truth.

Before I could jot down anything more, the taxi rattled down another stretch of bumpy cobblestones, jolting my notebook and skittering my pen across the page. I let out a frustrated sigh and snapped the notebook shut. There would be time enough to write it all down once I arrived home.

The instant the cab came to a halt in front of my residence, Mister Black swung open the door as though he'd been standing there all along, waiting for any sign of my return. A swell of gratitude and relief fluttered in my chest at his unwavering reliability.

"Is Lord Robert home?" I asked, handing him my coat, my voice still tight with the tension of the morning.

"No, milady. He telephoned to say he's attending the hearing before the magistrate. He won't return until early afternoon."

My stomach clenched. "Thank you, Mister Black," I managed. "I shall be in my parlor."

"Would you like coffee served?"

He knew my habits so well. "Yes, please," I replied, trying for a calm I didn't feel. "And a sandwich. Ham, I think, if Cook has one at the ready." I realized it was nearly noon and I'd barely eaten a thing.

A few minutes later, I made my way to the parlor, pausing only briefly to freshen up. The comforting scents of rich coffee and ham wafted toward me as I entered. Though the air in the room was warm from the fire in the hearth, I couldn't shake the chill of foreboding creeping along my spine. As I poured the coffee, my mind wandered back to Hollingsworth in that cold, claustrophobic cell. We had to find proof he wasn't the murderer.

I hadn't even finished my sandwich when the hall clock chimed one o'clock, and Robert appeared in the doorway. At first glance, I could tell all was not well—his shoulders were tight, and a heaviness darkened his usually steady gaze.

"How did the hearing go?" I asked quietly.

He exhaled, running a hand through his hair as though trying to rake away the tension. "The magistrate ruled there was sufficient evidence to charge Hollingsworth with Arkwright's murder. He's being held in Pentonville Prison, awaiting trial."

My heart twisted in my chest. Even though we'd feared this outcome, hearing it spoken aloud struck me like a blow. "I'm so sorry," I murmured. "Were you able to speak with him?"

"Yes." Robert's jaw tightened. "He was in good spirits, at least outwardly. Joking about the time he'd have to catch up on his reading. You know him. But he's worried."

"As are we. What did Sir Frederick say?"

"The case against Hollingsworth leaks like a sieve."

"How so?"

"Well, the witness who saw Hollingsworth supposedly arguing with Arkwright said the time was around three."

"Well, that couldn't have happened. Eloise was there. She would have seen it."

"Yes, but Bolton didn't have her testify. He only presented evidence that damned Hollingsworth."

My frustration flared. "Bolton seems to have a vendetta against Hollingsworth. Why?"

"Because Hollingworth's my best friend. I made a fool out of Bolton during the investigation into the Duke of Wynchcombe's murder. Ever since, he's been looking for a way to get back at me. With this murder, he found it."

"Do you think he planted that witness . . . what's her name again?"

"Maddie Parklane," Robert supplied, nearly spitting out the name.

"She's lying."

"I know she is. Not only would Eloise have seen her, but Hollingsworth was home at the time she claims he was arguing with Arkwright. His staff can swear to that."

"We have to find out who and what she is." I sighed even as I said it. One more thing to add to the list.

"Did you talk to Eloise?" he asked, raking a hand through his hair.

"Yes." I shared everything I'd learned.

"We need to provide Sir Frederick with Eloise's details. She'll need to testify at the trial."

A sense of panic set in. "Surely, it won't get to that point. We'll discover the murderer before then, won't we?"

"We have to be ready to present the best evidence we can to exonerate Hollingsworth."

"*We* have to present the best evidence?" Barristers were the ones to offer evidence for the defense, not Scotland Yard Inspectors. I sensed there was something he wasn't telling me.

"I've taken a leave of absence from Scotland Yard. Until this matter is resolved."

My throat tightened. I knew how difficult that decision must have been.

"I can't remain impartial," he admitted. "Hollingsworth isn't just a suspect to me—he's my friend. My best friend."

I slipped my arms around him, holding him close. "You did the right thing, darling."

He leaned into me, releasing a ragged breath, then brushed a tender kiss across my forehead. "On the way back, I visited my brother."

I looked up to find a shadow of grief in his eyes. "How is he?"

"No better," Robert said softly. "The doctor doesn't hold out much hope. He told me to prepare myself."

My heart clenched. "Oh, Robert." I squeezed him, wishing I could absorb his pain. "I'm so sorry."

Somewhere in the distance, the half-hour chimed. Reality persisted, marching ever forward.

"Have you eaten?" I asked, noticing how the stress had carved lines around his mouth.

He shook his head. "No. There was no time."

"Well," I said, managing a faint smile, "we can certainly remedy that."

I had the staff deliver some sustenance for him. Nothing fancy. But then he preferred that type of fare. While he ate, I avoided any discussion about the investigation. He was entitled to a moment of peace.

But much too soon our guests began to arrive, and we had to surge once more into the breach.

CHAPTER 17

THE SECOND MEETING OF THE INVESTIGATIVE COMMITTEE

Robert and I walked into the library to find everyone from yesterday's meeting present. Except for Richard, that is. He'd telephoned to say he would be arriving late. I was happy to see Emma and Mellie chatting away on the settee, smiles on both their faces. Ned and Marlowe were standing by the tall cabinet in the corner of the room, each with a drink in his hand. Going by their sober expressions, whatever they were discussing seemed to be of a serious nature.

"Good afternoon," I said. "Thank you for coming."

A chorus of 'Good afternoons' replied.

"Ned, Marlowe if you could take your seats, we will get started."

"Shouldn't we wait for Richard?" Ned asked as he and Marlowe accommodated themselves on brown leather chairs.

"He's running late, but he'll be here." Offering a smile, I said, "Hopefully, you had a productive morning."

"We did," Mellie exclaimed turning to Emma who nodded in agreement.

"That's wonderful, Mellie." I glanced down at the agenda. "I'd like to begin with Robert's report on the hearing." It would be best to get the bad news out of the way.

Emma must have anticipated what was to come because she held Mellie's hand while Robert provided his account. Everyone was appalled Hollingsworth had been charged with murder. Dear Mellie kept a stiff upper lip while he spoke, but her eyes quickly filled with tears.

"May I visit him at Pentonville?" Mellie asked. "I'd like him to know he's not alone. That we're fighting for him."

"I'm sure that can be arranged," Robert said in a kind voice.

"What about the other matter you were to investigate, Robert? Did you discover anything?"

"Yes, I did. They found poison in a tea tin adorned with Indian motifs. From the amount of tea remaining in the container, they estimated it had only been used the once."

"Once was all it would take, presumably," Ned said.

"Indeed, that was the medical examiner's opinion. I spoke with him. He found poison in Arkwright's stomach."

"So, there's no doubt that's what killed him?" Marlowe asked.

"None at all," Robert responded.

"Now that we know the origin of the poison," I said, "we need to determine who gave it to him." Before I could continue, Richard rushed in, windblown, pink-cheeked, and looking more alive than I'd seen him in the last several weeks. "My apologies for being late. What did I miss?"

Robert quickly summarized the information he'd shared.

"We were just about to shift our focus to the Mistletoe

Shoppe visit. Are you up to it, Mellie?" I had a particular reason for asking her to provide that report.

Firming up her chin, she said, "Yes, of course." After retrieving a notebook and clearing her throat, she said, "We were a half hour late getting started. One of us had a sartorial mishap."

"Marlowe, not me," Emma rushed to interject.

Marlowe shot Emma a mischievous glance. "What can I say? I'm a slave to fashion."

"He misplaced his tiepin," Emma said. "Again."

"At least this time you didn't have to go in search of it. I found it all by myself."

"Children." I clapped my hands. "Let us return to the topic at hand, shall we?"

"My apologies," Marlowe said. He didn't appear the least bit sorry.

"Please proceed, Mellie," I said.

"Once we arrived at the shop, we made our way to the alley behind the store. Thankfully, no one was around. Using the key we found hidden behind the waterspout, we were able to enter through the back door."

"How did you know it would be there?" I asked Robert as that knowledge could only have come from him.

"An old trick shop owners use. Learned that from my police patrolling days," he said. "I discovered the hidden key during my initial investigation into Arkwright's murder."

I turned back to Mellie. "Did you take care not to be seen while inside the store?"

"We didn't have to. The shop was shuttered up. No policeman was guarding it, either. We made sure of that before we made our move."

I suppressed a smile. *Made our move.* She already sounded like a detective.

"It was downright eerie, Kitty," she said softly. "The store may have been empty of customers. But all those smiling dolls . . ." She shuddered. "It felt like they would come to life any moment."

"I wound up a few toys for a look at their mechanisms," Marlowe admitted with a slightly mischievous grin. "One was a clockwork soldier that marched in place, and another was a tiny songbird that perched on a branch. That last one was not in the showroom. For whatever reason, it was in the back."

"When Marlowe wound up the bird," Emma added, her cheeks coloring with excitement, "it played a snippet from an aria. Mellie recognized the tune."

"It was from *Madama Butterfly*, a Puccini opera," Mellie said.

A strange thrill fluttered in my stomach. Figures she'd know. Mellie was not only a lover of music but practically a piano virtuoso.

"The bird. Was it perhaps a mechanical nightingale?"

"Yes," Emma said, tilting her head. "It was quite exquisite. Carved with delicate plumage and painted with gold filigree. The little bird's beak moved in time with the melody."

I drew a quiet breath. "A nightingale singing an aria. You're sure that's what it was?"

Mellie nodded. "Yes. It definitely was. There were several of them at the convent in France. Live ones, not mechanical, of course." After her mother became deadly ill, Mellie had been raised by nuns in a French convent. A year ago, after Mellie turned eighteen, Hollingsworth had brought her to London so she could make her debut. Although he'd arranged for a cousin to guide her through the season, she'd become incapacitated and unable to chaperone. And so, Mellie had come to live with the Worthington family. A happy day for everyone involved.

The mention of the mechanical singing bird had

prompted a fond memory. "We found that music box in Paris, darling," I said to Robert. "A ballerina. Do you remember?"

"Of course I do. I bought it for you."

"Yes, you did."

Robert and I exchanged an intimate glance as we recalled that visit to the Parisian shop. I don't know how long we would have remained that way if not for Marlowe. "Kitty! Robert! Lovebirds!"

That last word broke our connection. "What?"

"The matter at hand?" Marlowe reminded us.

"Oh, yes. Forgive me, er, us. Yes, well."

"I suppose she'll make sense at some point," Marlowe said.

"Oh, stow it, Marlowe," Emma said. "They've only been married for two months. They're allowed a loving glance or two."

Firmly back in the moment, I said, "Thank you, Emma. I apologize for the momentary lapse."

"Don't mention it."

"The mechanical nightingale is an important clue, I believe." I saw it bridging two distinct threads: the mention Hollingsworth had made of someone going by the code name Nightingale, and the existence of an actual mechanical nightingale in Arkwright's shop. It couldn't be a coincidence. Was the reference to a nightingale pointing us toward a woman who might be the key to this entire mystery? Even as excitement coursed through me, I reminded myself to be discrete, especially in front of Mellie. With a steady voice, I ventured, "It might tie in with something Hollingsworth learned."

Mellie shifted forward on the settee. "What do you mean? Who or what is nightingale?"

Before I could answer, Robert spoke gently. "Careful, darling," he warned me. "We can't divulge everything, especially not if it treads into territory that might be . . . sensitive."

"Right," I murmured. "Mellie, dear, for now, I can only say that there's a person known as Nightingale. She might be relevant. It's crucial we find more about her, especially if she has a connection to Arkwright and that tea tin."

Mellie's face expressed frustration, but she nodded. "All right," she said slowly. "If you believe it's better I do not know certain details, I respect that. But is there something I could do?"

"Indeed," Emma chimed in. "We're eager to help."

I turned to them both, seeking the right words. "Tomorrow, the two of you should go to *The Times* and ask for the reporter who covers theatre and opera—particularly during the war years. We need to find out if they know of a lady singer who traveled to France during that period."

Emma's mouth curved in a pleased smile. "Understood. We'll leave first thing in the morning."

Marlowe stirred in his seat. "I shall accompany them," he declared. "You can't have two charming ladies alone on Fleet Street unguarded."

Emma shot him a sidelong look. "We've guarded ourselves perfectly well before."

He grinned in response. "That you have. Nevertheless, I'd be rather bored left behind."

"You best be on time. If not, we'll leave without you." Emma turned to her new bosom friend. "Won't we, Mellie?"

"Indeed we will, Emma!" When she giggled, I was glad to see her smiling again.

As we were done with their report and they could not be privy to Ned's and Richard's, I dismissed them. But not before agreeing on our next meeting—the next day at two.

Once they'd gone, I pivoted toward Ned who had opened

his notebook and was scanning a few scribbles. "What news have you, dear brother?"

He grinned at my affectionate term probably because we hadn't always seen eye to eye. After he'd caught me in a dark garden with a titled gentleman hoping for my first kiss, I'd been sent away to a finishing school in Switzerland where Mother hoped I would gain a bit of polish and some common sense. I'd resented it, of course, and had blamed him for my banishment. But that experience had been exactly what I needed. After he escorted me back home, we'd reestablished our strong sibling connection. It hadn't hurt that I'd saved him from the noose.

"I had my meeting with Lord Peterson," Ned said. "We discussed investments—year-end performance, new opportunities in the new year, that sort of thing. I flattered him rather shamelessly, complimented the immaculate state of his attire and how thoroughly I admired his valet's skill. Lord Peterson lapped it up. He's arranged for me to meet his valet, Hargreaves, tomorrow at ten."

"That's excellent," I said, leaning forward in my chair. "Any sense that Hargreaves might be connected to Arkwright?"

Ned shook his head. "No direct sense yet. But Hollingsworth did mention him, if not by name. Perhaps there's something there. I'll do my best to pry out any relevant information. Subtly, of course."

I couldn't help a small laugh. "I'm sure you'll be very convincing, dear Ned." I glanced down at my notes. "Richard, why don't you share with us what you learned?"

Robert gestured for him to take a seat, but Richard waved it off, preferring to stand. "I found two old acquaintances," he began. "Both served on missions during the Great War. The talk drifted to codenames we used back then—some we recognized, some we didn't."

He took a breath and continued, "One chap recalled a woman who went by the name Nightingale. A singer. She was very popular with the Germans as she knew several Wagner arias. Additionally, there was mention of a valet known as "Passepartout". British but spoke French like a native."

"Another literary reference." It wasn't the first, someone in Intelligence had given Hollingsworth the code name Hook, the pirate in *Peter Pan*.

"Yes," Richard gave a dry chuckle.

The mention of Passepartout made me recall Eloise's fussbudget man: carefully dressed, mustache, and neat manner. Could that be the same person? My pulse quickened.

I glanced at Ned who was busy scribbling notes again.

"It seems Lord Peterson's valet might indeed be Passepartout." I shared what Eloise had told me.

"So, this man visited the Mistletoe Shoppe the day before he was murdered," Richard said.

"Yes. A woman, who might be Nightingale, and a man, who might be Passepartout. Anything else, you'd like to report? Ned, Richard?"

They both shook their heads.

"In that case," Robert suggested, "you should summarize our action plan, Catherine, so everyone is clear about how we will be moving forward."

"Yes, of course. Let's see." I glanced down at my notes. "Emma and Mellie, with Marlowe for company, will head to *The Times* tomorrow morning. Find out from the theatre correspondent if he knows of a singer or stage performer who sings operas, especially someone who traveled to France during the Great War."

"Ned," I continued, "your meeting with Lord Peterson's valet is tomorrow at ten. You will determine if he meets

Eloise's description. We know Lord Peterson traveled to France on several occasions. He has business interests there. So, we'll need to discover if his valet accompanied him."

"I can obtain that information from Peterson himself," Ned said. "No need to question the valet about it since it might alert him to our suspicions."

"Right you are," I said.

Ned tapped his pen against his notebook, a sure sign he felt energized by the challenge. "Don't worry. I'll be thorough. I know how to interrogate a suspect."

"Richard," I said, turning to him. "Could you follow up with your contacts? Any further details about the woman known as Nightingale might help us. Also, see if your contacts will provide you with more information on Passepartout."

He gave a brisk nod. "Of course. I've already arranged a second meeting at the club tomorrow morning with one of the chaps. He might recall more, once he's had time to rummage through his brainbox."

Finally, I glanced at Robert. "You'll be at Scotland Yard again, I presume?"

"Yes," he replied, his eyes meeting mine. "I'll press Bolton for details on the witness who claimed to see Hollingsworth. We need to question her ourselves, if possible."

"Absolutely," I said as a unanimous murmur of agreement filled the library.

"What about you?" Ned asked. "What will you be doing?"

"I will visit Salverton."

"He won't talk," Robert said.

"No, but I will."

CHAPTER 18

A DISCUSSION WITH SALVERTON

My meeting with Salverton did not get off to a splendid beginning. For starters, he was not home, but he was expected to return within the hour. I apologized profusely to his secretary, telling him I must have gotten the time wrong. Although he looked askance at my blatant lie, he had the butler show me to the drawing room to await Salverton's arrival.

His servants were everything a well-trained staff could be. I was served remarkably good coffee and a full array of sweets. I'd eaten so many of them during the last week, I'd gained weight, a rare occurrence for me.

Finally, after an hour, Salverton strolled through the door. The expression on his face did not augur well for our discussion. "Lady Robert, you shouldn't be here."

"How very welcoming of you."

"I didn't intend it to be." He blew out a breath. "It would

be beyond rude for me to show you to the door. But I will if I must."

"Don't you want to know what we've discovered? You did ask for my help."

"You know well and good I rescinded that request the last time I saw you."

"And you know well and good we wouldn't stop. Hollingsworth is Robert's best mate. And, if I recall correctly, he was your mate as well."

"Unfortunately, someone in my position does not have the luxury of having a best mate. All we're allowed are acquaintances."

"That makes for a very sad existence."

"My choice. Now, if you will." He pointed to the door.

"We know about Nightingale and Passepartout."

Much like Robert had done, Salverton faced the wall and offered a few choice expletives. They must have learned that while at Oxford. They both attended that august university.

Once he finished venting his spleen, he turned back toward me. "How did you discover this?"

Rather than answer, I said, "We believe both visited the Mistletoe Shoppe the day before Arkwright was murdered. Once we verify they in fact did, we will present all the evidence we've collected to Scotland Yard. Not Bolton, but the superintendent. He will more than likely charge one of them with murder. I imagine it will be made public at some point. Is that what you want?"

He brushed a hand across his brow. "Of course not. That might lead to the entire courier operation being out in the open. The couriers' covers would be blown. Their lives would be placed in danger." He paused for a moment to take a breath. "If you proceed with this, you and your husband will be taken into custody."

"I can just see it now. *Lord and Lady Robert apprehended.* Won't that make a pretty headline?"

"It'll never see the light of day."

"Oh, come now, Salverton. Of course, it will. You may control some of the press, but not all of them will bend the knee."

"They will when it puts national security in peril."

"So, stop it from getting there."

"What do you want from me?"

"I want you to tell me the identities of Nightingale and Passepartout. I want to see their photographs. You must have them stashed somewhere. And then I want you to set up a meeting with both. Tomorrow at seven at the safe house where we first discussed Lady Denton."

"And what reason shall I give for the meeting?"

"You'll think of something."

Silence reigned in the room while he pondered my demand. In the meantime, I calmly refreshed my cup and sipped from it.

Finally, after a full minute, he said, "The photos are confidential, you understand?"

I breathed a sigh of relief. He'd not only agreed but verified we were on the right track. "Of course. I wouldn't assume anything else."

"I'll present them to you in person. It will take an hour to retrieve them."

"I understand. Bring them to Eaton Square. I'll be expecting you." Having said what I came to say, I came to my feet. "Don't fail me, Salverton. If you do, I'll personally pass the information to *The Tattler*. They love me there, don't you know?"

"You will be clapped in irons if you do." He curled his upper lip. "Is he worth it?"

"I love my husband. He is my whole world."

"That's not who I meant."

"I know you didn't." After one last glance at the man who stood outraged in the center of the room, I walked out the door, satisfied with what I'd achieved.

∼

Thankfully, there was a cab stand close to where Salverton lived. So, it was only a matter of choosing one. Somehow, I'd managed not to shake until I climbed inside. But once I did, the tremors began.

The cab driver gave me an odd look, but all he did was ask, "Where to, ma'am?"

"Eaton Square, please."

I had maintained my poise while talking to Salverton even though I'd been quaking within the entire time. It was a gamble what I'd done. Robert would most surely have something to say. But we needed to know who Nightingale and Passepartout were. One of them was most surely the murderer. Now all we had to do was prove which one.

Once I arrived home, I headed for my bedchamber, not the one I shared with Robert, but my private one. Mother had suggested there'd be times when I wished for the privacy it would provide. This was one of those times. I rang for Grace who helped me into a much-needed bath. As much as I wished to linger, I really couldn't. Salverton would be here in an hour. It was nearly that time now. With Grace's help, I rushed through my toilette. Before long, I was toweled dry, powdered, and dressed. After a spritz of my favorite rose perfume, I descended the stairs to the library to find Robert had returned.

"You look beautiful, darling."

"Thank you."

"Needed a good soak, did you?" he asked with a grin.

"You know me so well." I offered my cheek for a kiss.

"How did it go with Salverton?"

I told Robert everything that happened, what I said, how Salverton responded. At the end of my recitation, his only comment was "Hmmmm."

"Hmmm? Is that all you have to say? I may just have landed us in jail."

"You haven't." Embracing me, he moved me side to side in his arms, almost like we were dancing.

I soon put a stop to the nonsense and glared at him. "How do you know?"

"Salverton has more sense than that. If we were clapped in irons, the papers would find out. Conspiracy theories would soon be flying about and the story would not die down. If there is one thing that intelligence prizes above just about everything is secrecy. They can't afford the notoriety." He brushed his lips against mine. "You did the right thing."

I practically collapsed with relief. "If I'd known you'd take it so well, I would not have worried so much."

"Ahem." Our butler stood at the library door. "Sorry to interrupt, Lord Robert, Lady Robert."

"Yes, Mister Black," Robert said.

"Lord Salverton wishes for a moment of your time."

"Please show him in," I said.

In no time at all, Salverton strode into the library, his temper still high, going by his ruddy cheeks. Although it could have been the blustery wind, I didn't think so.

Having done his duty, Mister Black promptly withdrew, closing the door behind him.

"What a pleasure to see you again, Salverton!" Robert said with a wide grin which I fully echoed.

"You two are as mad as hatters!"

"That's why we're so well suited." I placed my palm on Robert's chest. "Aren't we, darling?"

He cupped his hand over mine. "Right you are, precious!"

All we got from Salverton was a raised brow.

"Did you bring what I requested?" I asked.

By way of answer, he reached into his coat and retrieved a small brown envelope. "The names and photographs are inside." And then he handed it to me.

After carefully opening the envelope, I removed the contents. Two names were written on a plain white sheet of paper. *Rafaella Rossini* and *Joseph Hargreaves*. The first was new to us but we knew the second. "Can you see, darling?" I asked Robert who stood behind me looking over my shoulder.

"Yes."

The photographs showed a gentleman and a lady who exactly matched the descriptions Eloise had given me of the two individuals who had visited the shop, down to the man's mustache and the lady's generous proportions.

"I'll need the photos back. You can burn the paper."

"Of course," I said handing the images back to him.

"I trust that's all you need?"

"Except for the meeting."

"That's being arranged. Shouldn't pose a problem. They're both in town. How do you intend to determine which one is the murderer?"

"I have my ways."

"You will let me know how you proceed. I'll need to arrange things."

"We will. Thank you, Salverton. We'll see you tomorrow."

Without another word, he performed a turnabout and left.

"That's not a happy chappie," Robert said.

"Indeed." I glanced up at him. "Have you eaten?"

"No."

I curled my arm around his elbow. "Let us have a proper luncheon then. In the morning room, I think."

"Whatever you say, darling."

Luncheon consisted of a salad made up of fresh, crisp greens, radishes, tomatoes, cucumbers, and artichokes tossed with a light vinaigrette. The meat course was roast beef, accompanied by a side of asparagus. For dessert, Cook treated us to slices of a scrumptious chocolate genoise cake.

Robert ate every bite. I, on the other hand . . .

"You barely touched your food," Robert commented.

"Salverton's staff brought out some rather delicious treats while I waited for him. Nervous as I was, I ate more than I should have." I patted my stomach. "If I'm not careful, I'll grow round as a berry."

Propping his chin on his palm, he grinned at me. "That just means there'll be more of you to love."

"Flatterer." I dropped my napkin on the table and came to my feet. "Shall we take our coffee in the library? It's almost time for the meeting to start."

"Wherever you go, I will follow."

I rolled my eyes at him as we drifted out of the morning room. "Don't you start! It's nauseating enough to hear such nonsense from Marlowe."

"The man is in love."

"I know, but he doesn't have to be so sickening about it. How Emma can stand it . . ."

"Did I hear my name?" Emma. In the flesh. In our foyer. Marlowe and Mellie as well. They all were sporting wide grins.

Bother! They'd all heard me. Well, there was only one way to deal with that *faux pas*. Ignore it. "You've arrived. How wonderful! Shall we proceed to the library?"

Of course, Marlowe couldn't pass that up. "Where thou goest—"

"Hush!" Emma exclaimed in a loud whisper.

CHAPTER 19

THIRD MEETING OF THE INVESTIGATIVE COMMITTEE

I led the way to the library where our wonderful staff had set up the coffee and tea service, as well as an assortment of pastries. I'd have to abstain from the latter, but coffee would not go amiss. I'd need it to remain awake, as I was in desperate need of a nap. No wonder. I'd hardly slept a wink last night.

"So how did it go at *The Times*?" I asked once everyone had a chance to help themselves to the refreshments.

"Let's wait until Ned and Richard are present," Robert suggested.

"Well, then you may proceed," Ned said strolling into the room, "for we have arrived." Richard was right on his heels.

"First of all, I want to thank all of you for your assistance. You didn't have to heed the call, but you did. Robert and I, and Hollingsworth, if I may speak for him, are extremely grateful you did."

"No need to thank us, Kitty," Emma said. "You know how much we enjoy doing this."

A chorus of "Hear! Hear!" circled the room.

Folding my hands in front of me, I said, "Mellie, why don't you get us started?"

Her cheeks pinked up. "I spoke last time. Maybe Emma should do it today?"

"And miss your wonderful summation?" Emma said, shaking her head. "I don't think so. You noted down every detail at the newspaper. If I were to do it, I'm sure I'd miss a point or two."

One of the things about Emma was that she had a mind like a steel trap. She could recall conversations from several years ago without jotting down one single word.

"Well, if you insist," Mellie said.

"I do. Go on," Emma said.

"We arrived at ten. Having telephoned the day before, there was a gentleman waiting for us—the entertainment critic, Mister Stafford. He'd been with the newspaper for the last twenty years. So, he was very familiar with the theatre scene. He indeed knew of an opera singer who often traveled to France during the Great War, a soprano by the name of Rafaella Rossini. He showed us a photograph of her. She'd even autographed it. The lady was everything the shop girl described."

"How wonderful you've done, Mellie!"

"She married a very wealthy man, an admirer who never missed a performance in London. He presented her with a dozen red roses every night. According to him, her marriage is a success. We know her married name. It shouldn't be a problem to track her down."

"Indeed, it should be a rather easy task," Emma said. She turned her gaze toward me, and a question suddenly materialized in her eyes. "Is that no longer necessary?"

Leave it to her to realize something had changed. "We've found another way to reach her. Arrangements have been made."

Mellie's shoulders drooped. My words had taken the wind out of her sails. Poor thing appeared so crestfallen I simply had to say, "You've done a great job, Mellie. You should be proud of yourself."

She sighed. "But it didn't do any good. It didn't help."

"You're wrong. It did. You've verified we're on the right track."

"Truly?" she asked with a glint of hope in her gaze.

"Truly," I said.

In an instant, Mellie's mood lifted. "Then I'm glad."

Emma squeezed her hand. "As well you should be."

"Now that that has been settled, Ned please tell us what you found."

He glanced toward Emma, Marlowe, and Mellie, "Should they be hearing what I have to say?"

"You can discuss it without naming names, can't you?"

"Well, yes, but I'd prefer not to. Questions will arise."

"He's right, darling," Robert said.

"Very well." I gazed at the group Ned had named. "It seems you'll need to leave."

Marlowe practically jumped to his feet. "May I escort you ladies back to the Worthington residence?"

"Thank you, Marlowe." Emma extended her hand to Mellie. "Ready?"

"Of course," Mellie said taking it. "If you need anything else," she said, gazing at me, "let me know."

"I will thank you, Mellie. You as well, Emma, and finally, Marlowe. Your efforts are truly appreciated."

Emma wrapped an arm around Mellie's shoulders. "Once we get to Worthington House, I have a secret to share with you."

"What is it?" Mellie said, brightening up.

"Not here," Emma said with a secretive grin. "You'll find out soon enough."

It was a much happier Mellie that walked out of the room.

"What was that all about?" Richard asked.

"I have a pretty good idea, not that I've been made privy to it. Now Ned, tell us what you found."

"Well, the valet's name is Joseph Hargreaves. But I gather you already know. He meets the shop girl's description. After he shared his sartorial expertise, I told him our investment firm had several clients in the continent, and I was concerned my current wardrobe would be seen as passe there. That's all it took for him to wax lyrical about the various designers, especially the Italian and French ones. Apparently, he traveled extensively with Lord Peterson. So, he had an opportunity to see what the gentlemen wore, especially in France. He never traveled to Germany, though. Lord Peterson's business interests only took them to Italy and France."

"Did he seem cagey or secretive?"

"No. He spoke with a great deal of enthusiasm and was very receptive to my questions."

"Could he be the murderer?"

"I didn't see any guile in him. So, no. I don't think it was him."

I had to trust Ned's opinion. He was an excellent judge of character. "Thank you, Ned. What about you, Richard? What did you find?"

"I spent most of the morning at the Explorers Club without much success. But just as I was about to leave, I ran into one of my former mates. Now, he was a secretive chap and extremely bright. I was surprised to learn he'd sought me out."

"Interesting," I said. "What did he have to say?"

"He'd made the connection between Arkwright's murder and the questions I'd been asking around the club. We sought out a private spot where we could talk without being overheard. Turns out he'd been one of the couriers. Could have knocked me over with a feather. I never suspected it of him. He was born with a silver spoon in his mouth, so he had no need to jump into the fray as it were. But he felt he had to do his bit for King and Country. So he volunteered. He also has a facility for languages."

"Same as you."

"Yes. Well, he told me about this one courier. Odd sort of chap. Walked with a limp. Spoke German like a true native. He was sent into the Motherland herself. One time he spotted the chap in a place he shouldn't have been, talking to a high-ranking German officer. When my mate returned to England, he reported it to his superior. Next thing he knew, his services were terminated. He was never sent on another mission again."

"That's odd, isn't it?" I asked.

"Maybe he saw something he shouldn't have seen," Ned suggested.

"Or maybe something nefarious was happening within the Intelligence department," Robert said. "We'll need to ask Salverton about this courier when we see him tonight."

"You managed to talk to him, Kitty?" Ned asked.

"Indeed, I did." I shared what I'd told Salverton and the things I'd demanded from him.

"And he agreed?"

"He did."

Ned shook his head. "That could have gone very wrong, Kitty."

"But it didn't. Tonight, we should be able to determine who the murderer is."

CHAPTER 20

A MURDERER UNMASKED

Sometime later, Robert and I headed to the safe house where we would be meeting with Salverton and the two couriers. Whatever the outcome, we'd agreed to share it with Ned and Richard, but not Emma, Mellie, and Marlowe. Hopefully, the only news they'd learned would be that Hollingsworth had been released.

We arrived a few minutes early to discover the other invitees were already there. Rafaella Rossini was a stunning beauty. No one had mentioned that. Her dark tresses had been cleverly arranged into a braided crown adorned with diamanté stars. Her dark eyes gleamed with curiosity more than anything else. Joseph Hargreaves, on the other hand, appeared quite perplexed as to the reason for his presence.

As soon as Robert and I took our seats, Salverton took command of the gathering. "Nightingale, Passepartout, I have asked you here tonight to clear up certain matters regarding the murder of Mister Arkwright, the Mistletoe Shoppe owner."

Madame Rossini's expression grew somber. "So sad. Who would do that to such a wonderful man?"

Hargreaves did not say a word but suddenly appeared very nervous.

"Just so," Salverton said. "I will now turn the meeting over to Lady Marigold who will explain things."

I came to my feet, "Thank you, er, Bunny." I had no idea if the two couriers knew his real identity. But since he'd used my code name, I decided to do the same. "Nightingale, Passepartout, we have been reliably informed you both visited the Mistletoe Shoppe the day before Mister Arkwright was murdered. Is that correct?"

Both nodded but Madame Rossini was the only one to speak. "Indeed, it was so. I brought him a holiday gift."

"And what was that gift?"

"A mechanical nightingale. It trilled the opening notes of an aria from *Madama Butterfly*. I thought it would amuse him." She proceeded to sing a snippet.

"You have a beautiful voice, Nightingale," I said.

"Merci, madame. I used to sing professionally. I no longer do. Life has taken me in another direction."

"A shame such a gift is no longer heard."

She nodded. *"Mais oui."*

Clearly, she was not the murderer. So it could only be the other courier. I turned to him. "Passepartout, did you, in fact, also visit the Mistletoe Shoppe?"

He nodded. "I did. I also brought a gift."

"And what was it?" I sensed anticipating closing the trap.

"A tin of tobacco."

"Tobacco?" Well, that was entirely unexpected.

"Yes. Arkwright smoked a pipe. He preferred Cuban tobacco. Very hard to find and very expensive. But I found a shop that carried it—Royal Briar & Smoke. It also sells very fine pipes, but they were beyond my budget. So, I chose the tobacco—Habana Oro."

I gazed at Robert with astonishment. Not only was it the same shop I'd bought tobacco for Mister Black, but it was the same brand.

"Are you sure?"

"Of course, I'm sure. Cost me a pretty bob. I still have the receipt if you need to see it." From the depths of his coat, he retrieved a small sheet of paper and handed it to me. It verified what he'd told me.

I passed it to Robert. Within seconds, he murmured, "Excuse us," and pulled me out of the room. "We found a tin of that tobacco on the premises. We tested it, of course. At the time, we had no idea what had caused Arkwright's death."

"I gather you didn't find poison in that tin," I said.

"No. Only in the tea one."

"Neither of them killed Arkwright then." I couldn't help the disappointment in my voice. We were right back to square one.

Robert nodded. "It appears so."

"Who else could it have been?" I asked. Despondent did not begin to describe how I felt.

Suddenly, the door behind us opened and Salverton called out, "Lady Marigold. We may have found a lead."

Robert and I rushed back inside.

"Passepartout, tell Lady Marigold what you saw."

"The afternoon I came to the shop, I saw someone I recognized. A courier, same as me. I gather that's the connection since Nightingale and I both were?" He directed the question to Salverton who simply nodded.

"Who did you see?"

"I don't know his name, but we called him 'Kraut' because he spoke fluent German. Walks with a limp. He didn't see me as I'd already left the shop, but he strolled right in. He was welcomed right enough by the shop girl. Her grin was a mile wide when she spotted him."

A bad feeling came over me. It couldn't be who I thought it was. "What's his first name?" I asked Passepartout.

"Never knew it."

"Albert. His name is Albert," Salverton said.

I gazed in horror at Robert. "We have to go."

"I'm going with you," Salverton said.

"No."

"Whatever happens, I need to be there."

"He's right," Robert said. Turning to Salverton, he said, "My motorcar's outside."

On our way out, I turned back to Nightingale and Passepartout. "Thank you."

"Don't mention it, Cherie. Happy hunting!" Nightingale said.

"Get the bugger!" Passepartout said.

Bright lights gleamed in their eyes.

"Where to?" Robert asked once the three of us had climbed into the Rolls Royce.

"Eloise's flat. You know the address."

"Yes." It took over half an hour to get there. But we used the time strategizing how we would proceed once we arrived. I would be the one to knock on the door. They would remain at the entrance below. Once Eloise admitted me, I would ask her about Bertie, her sweetheart, to determine if he was the man Passepartout had identified. At that point, Salverton and Robert would take over the interrogation to find his whereabouts.

As it turned out, we didn't have to ask her about the latter. When I quietly climbed the steps to her residence, it was clear an argument was underway in her flat, loud enough to be heard through the thin walls.

"What did you tell the coppers, Ellie?" a male voice demanded.

"Nothing, Bertie. I didn't tell them a thing."

"You told someone else, though, didn't you about the tea tin."

"Miss Worthington. She was ever so nice. I told her about Arkwright's visitors. That one of them had given him the tin with the Indian drawings on it. I never mentioned your name. At least not when it came to the tea tin."

"You told her about us?"

"I told her we were sweethearts, and we were getting married, and you wanted me to move to my sister's house. But that's all I said."

"Miss Worthington? Who is she?"

"A lady detective. She gave me her card." After a moment or two, she said, "Here."

"Ladies of Distinction Detective Agency! That's the mort that's been in all the papers. She's married to a bleedin' detective inspector from Scotland Yard. That's who you told?"

"She didn't say anything about a detective inspector, Bertie. Why are you so angry at me?"

"You should have kept your mouth shut. You shouldn't have said anything."

"She wants to find out who killed Mister Arkwright, Bertie. What's wrong with talking to her?"

"Because they'll find out, that's why."

"Find out what?"

"That I gave him that tin of tea."

"When did you do that? I never saw you."

"I left it on the counter for him with a note. 'From a friend,' I wrote on it. He never knew it came from me."

"Why didn't you want him to know? That was such a nice thing to do."

"Because he was going to tell on me, that's why. He found out something I'd done during the Great War. Something bad."

"What did you do, Bertie?" Elsie's voice sounded apprehensive.

"I was a secret agent, Ellie," he said in a conspiratorial whisper.

She laughed. "You a secret agent? Go on with you. You're putting me on!"

"It's true. I was. British Intelligence chose me because I speak German like a native, because of my mother. That's where she was born. They sent me to France and Germany to deliver communiques. That's what they called them."

"But you didn't deliver them?"

"Oh, I did that all right. But not before I read them. We were not supposed to do that. I copied the information onto another communique. I'd stolen some of their fancy papers to make them look real, you see. And then I passed them to a German officer. He was really glad to have them, too. Made me a bob or two every time I gave him one of those. What a lark that was!"

For a moment, there was silence. And then Ellie asked, "What did you put in that tin, Bertie?"

"Tea, of course. From India, the real fancy stuff."

"What else?"

"That stuff you use to kill rats, blended it in really well. I bet he didn't know it was there. Until he started dying."

I stepped aside and allowed Robert and Salverton to rush into Ellie's flat. There was a brief scuffle and screams, but the end was predetermined. In no time at all, they were dragging Bertie down the stairs and out of the building.

I entered Eloise's flat to find her sitting on the bare floor, surrounded by boxes, weeping as if her heart was breaking.

"I'm so sorry, Eloise." Her happy dream of a wedding had ended.

"How could he kill Mister Arkwright? He was such a good man."

"I know, sweetheart. I know."

The rest of the evening passed in a blur. I remained with Eloise while she was questioned First by Robert and Bolton later on. But once the interrogation was finished, I insisted she be escorted to her sister's house. She was innocent in all of this and shouldn't have to be punished for what Bertie had done.

Robert saw to it that the door to her flat was secured, and then finally, he and I were allowed to go home.

CHAPTER 21

A QUIET FAREWELL

The days that followed were a flurry of activity. Hollingsworth was promptly released followed by an official announcement from Scotland Yard that the true murderer had been apprehended. Even though the press clamored for the name, none was given. Salverton had ensured no news about the courier network reached the news.

Bolton was placed on temporary suspension. His return to Scotland Yard was dubious at best. Not only had his slipshod investigation led to a wrongful arrest, but it had almost caused a national calamity. The witness who'd sworn under oath that she'd spotted Hollingsworth arguing with Cartwright had supposedly confused Hollingsworth with Bertie. Never mind the two men did not resemble each other in the least. The feeling at Scotland Yard was that Bolton had coached the witness to name Hollingsworth.

I shared with Emma, Marlowe, and Mellie what I could. They were satisfied with the resolution, especially Mellie. Her brother was a free man and that was all she cared about.

Mister Arkwright's will was a surprise. He'd left the shop to Eloise. She promised to continue the fine tradition Mister Arkwright had begun and was planning to reopen the shop in time for Epiphany, the day the Three Kings offered their gifts to the baby Jesus. She couldn't have chosen a better date. When I asked her opinion about the cup of tea Arkwright had drunk, she guessed he'd prepared it himself. Apparently, he often did that after a long day. Of course, we'd never know the truth. It would make no matter when it came to Bertie's guilt. He would still hang. The Crown Prosecutor would see to that.

As far as the marionette, Hollingsworth believed Arkwright had carved his name as a warning, not as a condemnation. Lady Denton had already warned Arkwright to beware. Once the effects of the poison made themselves known, he must have realized he was dying. With the little time he had left, he'd carved Hollingsworth's name into the marionette, not realizing it would damn Hollingsworth. Again, all conjecture.

As we approached New Year's Eve and Mother's celebration, there was one thing I needed to do even though it would go against someone's wishes. But I did not wish the year to end without visiting Robert's brother. I dressed in a festive gown, donned the pearl necklace he'd given me for my twenty-first birthday, and sailed out the door. Robert had gone to Scotland Yard so he wouldn't know until he returned.

I was kept waiting for half an hour in the drawing room of Rutledge House while Lord Rutledge's attendant made him ready for company. But finally, I was shown into his bedchamber. The change in him was enough to break my heart. The distinguished gentleman I'd always known was a mere husk of himself. I refused to show any darkness. Instead, I brought lightness and humor into that dark room.

"You shouldn't have come," Lord Rutledge said in a shaky voice after I walked into the room.

"I wanted to wish you a Happy New Year. It's only a day away."

"I might not live to see it."

"You will."

"How do you know?"

"Because it's my heart's fondest desire."

A weak laugh wheezed from him which soon turned into a coughing fit.

His attendant, who'd been standing at the ready, quickly put a glass of water to his lips.

"Not too much longer, Lady Robert," his attendant said. "His heart can't stand the strain."

"Yes, of course." Leaning over Lord Rutledge, I whispered a few words that brought a smile to his lips.

"Not my name. Our father's."

"Our son will bear your name."

"Aloysius?"

"Is that what it is?" I really should have checked before making the offer.

"Yes. Michael would be a better choice. It's a family name."

"Then that's what it'll be."

"Thank you for coming, my dear. You did an old man a world of good."

"I'm glad I did. Now don't you go dancing the night away tomorrow."

This time he didn't laugh but simply squeezed my hand.

"Goodbye, Aloysius."

His voice was faint, but I heard it clearly. "Goodbye, my dear. Take good care of my brother."

"I will." And with that, I departed. I would indeed care for Robert all the rest of my days. I would give him a son to be proud of. Not right away, of course. There were too many things I wanted to do. But soon.

CHAPTER 22

ALL'S WELL THAT ENDS WELL

New Year's Eve found us all at Worthington House. The entire Worthington family was there, even Margaret and Sebastian. My sister had convinced her husband to return to London as she wished to celebrate the New Year with the rest of her family, as well as him, of course.

In the matter of the menu, Mother had outdone herself. Working with Cook, she'd arranged a wonderful feast for us which consisted of cream of celery soup, poached Dover sole with white wine sauce, roast saddle of lamb served with mint sauce, accompanied by roasted potatoes and braised winter vegetables. For dessert Cook treated us to Charlotte Russe. When we finished the delicious meal, we withdrew to the drawing room to enjoy coffee, tea, and liqueurs. At midnight, champagne would be served to toast the New Year.

As I dropped next to Robert on the sofa, I said, "I don't

think I'll eat for a week. That meal was positively scrumptious."

He smiled as he curled his arm around my shoulders. "I'll remind you of that tomorrow at breakfast."

I gazed at Hollingsworth who stood by the hearth, enjoying the felicitations being tossed his way. But even though he was smiling, I sensed a deep sadness within him. "He puts up a good front, doesn't he?"

"You don't think he's happy?"

"He's happy he's out of jail, but something is bothering him." I gazed at Robert. "You wouldn't happen to know what it is?"

Robert shook his head. "He hasn't confided in me."

"Well, there's no time like the present to find out."

As I came to my feet, Robert held onto my hand, "Catherine, you shouldn't pry. Leave well enough alone. If he wishes to share what's troubling him, he will do so."

I thought about it for a moment or two, "You're right. It's just . . . I want him to be happy."

"You can't fix all the ills of the world, my darling." He raised my hand to his lips for a kiss.

"Attention, everyone!" Marlowe stood in the center of the room with Emma by his side, their hands entwined. When everyone's eyes were on him, he declared, "Lady Emma Carlyle has agreed to make me the happiest of men. We are to be married!"

The congratulations poured in, with the men pumping Marlowe's hand or slapping him on the back. The women embraced Emma and kissed her cheek. Robert and I waited until the surcease of excitement died down before approaching them.

"Congratulations, Marlowe," Robert said. "She finally made an honest man out of you."

"That remains to be determined," Emma answered with a laugh.

"I'm so happy for you both," I said, embracing Emma. "You are so well suited for each other."

"Thank you, Kitty. Yes, I think we are." She took me aside and whispered. "I will continue my work at the Ladies of Distinction Detective Agency. He finally realized how important that is to me."

"He's a good man, Emma, and he clearly adores you."

She blushed. One of the rare times she did. "Yes, well."

"And you clearly adore him. When's the wedding?"

"In the fall, I think. We must allow Lily her moment, shouldn't we?"

"Yes, we should."

"I would like you to be my matron of honour."

"I will be happy to do so."

"And Mellie one of the attendants?"

"She'll love it. Speaking of Mellie—"

"You don't have to say it. She's the one you're recommending for the new assistant detective position."

"She is."

"She conducted herself very well during this investigation. She's raw but has talent, as well as a wonderful spirit." Emma squeezed my hand. "We'll have to train her up a bit, but I think she will do fine."

"I agree."

"Hey, you two," Marlowe said approaching us, "Are you conspiring against me?"

Emma glanced at him. "Maybe. I'll need all the help I can get."

"You don't need any help." He raised her hand and kissed the palm. "You do just fine by yourself."

I left the two lovebirds making eyes at each other and approached Hollingsworth.

"I haven't had a chance to talk to you tonight. How are you? Really?"

He glanced toward his sister before returning his gaze to me. "I believe I'll take a holiday after the new year. Somewhere warm, I think, away from the cold."

"Your shoulder still bothering you?" He'd been shot while we conducted an investigation in Brighton. Although the wound had healed, the internal damage remained. As a sailor, he needed full use of his arm. That had to be the cause of his sadness, not that he'd admit it.

"Yes." And that's all he said.

"You will let Robert and I know before you leave."

"I will. Thank you for everything you did. I'm deeply aware of the risk you took. I can never repay you or Robert."

"You don't have to repay us, Hollingsworth. That's what friends are for."

A sad sort of smile flitted across his lips.

"Hey, everyone, it's almost midnight," Richard said. "Grab a glass of champagne." Almost overnight, he'd become a different person. The investigation had done him a world of good. Clearly, the key to his mental well-being was to find something useful to do. Father had once more suggested he talk to the curator at the British Museum about a position there. And this time, Richard agreed to do so. With any luck, he would become the man he once was.

Our footmen strolled around the room carrying trays of champagne flutes. But before I could grab one, Robert brought a glass to me. "Hollingsworth." He nodded toward his best friend.

"Robert." He nodded back. "Excuse me, I must find Mellie."

"Of course," I said.

Richard started the countdown. "Ten, nine, eight, seven, six . . .

When the clock struck twelve, Robert said, "Happy New Year, darling." And then he kissed me, and all the world faded away.

DID you enjoy **Murder in the Mistletoe Shoppe?** Read on to discover Kitty Worthington's next adventure, Murder at the British Museum.

A brutal murder. A brother charged with the crime. Can Kitty Worthington find the killer before he pays with his life?

Kitty Worthington couldn't be happier. Her marriage to CDI Robert Crawford Sinclair is glorious, her detective agency is thriving, and her brother Richard is on the mend after a close brush with death.

Now permanently home from his archeological excavations, Richard has taken a position at the British Museum. His lectures on Egyptian antiquities and the mummification process draw patrons like moths to a flame. But when he suspects several items in the Egyptian collection were stolen, he confronts the acquisitions curator. Outraged by the accusation, the official terminates his employment. Days later, the curator's gruesome remains are found, mummified.

It doesn't take long for suspicion to fall on Richard. Not

only is he an expert on mummification, but he has no alibi for the time of the murder. Fearing what will happen if he's charged with the crime, Kitty sets out to prove his innocence. Soon, she discovers the curator is not who he seems to be. As she stumbles into a world of strange cults and idol worship, she encounters a mesmerizing creature who leads her down a path to darkness. And death.

Murder at the British Museum, Book 11 in The Kitty Worthington Mysteries, is another captivating historical cozy mystery from the pen of *USA Today* Bestselling Author Magda Alexander. This riveting tale is sure to thrill you and keep you up at night.

∽

**Exciting New Series
By Magda Alexander**

From the pen of *USA Today* Bestselling Author Magda Alexander comes a new captivating Victorian historical mystery, A Murder in Mayfair, Book 1 in **The Lady Rosalynd and Steele Mysteries**.

A brutal murder. A reluctant alliance. Can an arrogant duke and a passionate reformer find a killer before their loved ones are condemned to the gallows?

London. 1889. Lady Rosalynd Rosehaven. Fierce advocate of women's causes. As guardian of her brothers and sisters, she considers herself a spinster. The Duke of Steele. A leader in the House of Lords. After the tragic death of his wife, he's sworn to remain a widower. Although they once worked together to find a stolen necklace, their paths are not likely to cross again.

But when her cousin is suspected of her husband's murder, and the duke's brother is implicated as well, Steele suggests they join forces to investigate the killing. Such an alliance would upset Rosalynd's well-ordered life. She'd found the duke arrogant, aloof, and . . . fascinating. However, she has no choice but to accept his offer. Proving her cousin's innocence takes precedence over her nonsensical misgivings.

As they track down clues from the opulent mansions of Mayfair to the sordid streets of St. Giles, they don't lack for suspects. Few had a good opinion of the victim who was considered a swindler, a card sharp, and worse. When a clue comes to light that leads to her cousin's arrest, Rosalynd embarks on a dangerous course. Can the duke stop her mad quest before she pays with her life?

Fans of the Bow Street Duchess Mysteries and the Angus Brodie & Mikaela Forsythe series will love **A Murder in Mayfair,** Book 1 in The Lady Rosalynd and Steele Mysteries.

CAST OF CHARACTERS

KITTY WORTHINGTON - OUR SLEUTH

THE LADIES OF DISTINCTION DETECTIVE AGENCY

Lady Emma Carlyle - Kitty's friend and partner in the Ladies of Distinction Detective Agency

Lady Aurelia Holmes - Assistant lady detective

Betsy Robson - Receptionist and assistant bookkeeper at the Ladies of Distinction Detective Agency, formerly Kitty's personal maid

Owen Clapham - former Scotland Yard detective inspector, aids with investigations

THE SINCLAIR FAMILY

Robert Crawford Sinclair - Kitty's Husband, a Scotland Yard Detective Chief Inspector. As the brother and presumptive

CAST OF CHARACTERS

heir to Lord Rutledge, he is formally referred to as Lord Robert by his staff
    Lord Rutledge - Robert's older brother, a marquis

THE CRAWFORD SINCLAIR HOUSEHOLD

Mister Black - the Crawford Sinclair butler
    Hudson - Robert's valet
    Grace Flanagan- Kitty's lady's maid

THE WORTHINGTON FAMILY

Mildred Worthington - Kitty's mother
    Edward Worthington - Kitty's father
    Ned Worthington - Kitty's oldest brother, engaged to Lily Dalrymple
    Richard Worthington - Kitty's next oldest brother, formerly in Egypt now in London

THE WORTHINGTON HOUSEHOLD

Carlton - the family butler
    Neville - the family chauffeur and Betsy's beau
    Sir Winston - Family's beloved basset hound

THE WYNCHCOMBE FAMILY AND HOUSEHOLD

His Grace the Duke of Wynchcombe, Sebastian Dalrymple - married to Margaret, Kitty's sister
    Her Grace the Duchess of Wynchcombe, Margaret Dalrymple - Kitty's older sister, now married to the Duke of Wynchcombe
    Lady Lily Dalrymple - Sebastian's sister, engaged to Ned, Kitty's brother, currently living with the Worthington family

OTHER NOTABLE CHARACTERS

Lord Hollingsworth - A marquis, explorer and adventurer, and Robert Crawford Sinclair's best mate

Lady Melissande ("Mellie") - Lord Hollingsworth's sister, currently living with the Worthington family

Lord Marlowe - An earl - Attracted to Lady Emma

Eloise - The Mistletoe Shoppe sales assistant

Bertie - Eloise's sweetheart

Lord Salverton - A marquis – Friend of Lord Hollingsworth, in the Intelligence business

Lady Delphine – A friend of Kitty's, owner of a modiste shop

This book is a work of fiction. All names, characters, locations, and incidents are products of the author's imagination, or have been used fictitiously. Any resemblance to actual persons living or dead, locales, or events is entirely coincidental.

Copyright © 2025 by Amalia Villalba

All rights reserved.

The uploading, scanning, and distribution of this book in any form or by any means—including but not limited to electronic, mechanical, photocopying, recording, or otherwise—without the permission of the copyright holder is illegal and punishable by law. Please purchase only authorized editions of this work, and do not participate in or encourage electronic piracy of copyrighted materials. Your support of the author's rights is appreciated.

ISBN-13: (EBook) 978-1-943321-36-0

ISBN-13: (Print) 978-1-943321-44-5

Hearts Afire Publishing

First Edition: January 2025

Made in United States
North Haven, CT
02 February 2025